Patchwork

**A Novel
by
Dan Loughry**

New York
Harvard Square Editions (HSE), Ltd.
www.HarvardSquareEditions.org
2011

Published in the United States by
Harvard Square Editions (HSE), Ltd.

ISBN: 978-0-9833216-1-3

Harvard Square Editions web address:
www.harvardsquareeditions.org

Printed in the United States of America

For my family: Dan, Vita, Mark and Frank;
and in memory of the millions

Part One

1989

"The dead have their own tasks."

— Rainer Maria Rilke

Patchwork
Part One; Chapter One

"**LET A LITTLE** light in, would you?" Sal asked. He was washing breakfast dishes in the kitchen while peering into the dark living room where his lover, weak with AIDS, sat quietly.

Randy, rising slowly, drew the curtains back. The brash sunlight — so quick, so harsh — dizzied him. He rested back on the sofa, a stiff vinyl monstrosity, and re-arranged the fake tiger throw-pillows against his lower back for support. He flipped on the TV with the remote control. Plinking new wave music played through the television speakers; some late 80's group with their current video.

"Your parents will be here in less than an hour," Sal said. "What are you doing?"

"Still dying."

"Well, before you drop that mortal coil," Sal hissed, "maybe you could dust."

Randy ignored him and continued watching TV.

A yellow Fiestaware cup wobbled as Sal placed it on the wooden drying rack. He felt an urge to smash the mug on the floor at Randy's feet. *Maybe then he'd move,* Sal thought. He propped his finger against the cup, ceasing its motion. "I cook, take care of you — "

"Do you bring home the bacon and fry it up in a pan?"

Exasperated, Sal placed his hands on his hips.

"Of course you do," Randy said, watching soap suds drip from Sal's elegant fingers, "'cause you're a woman."

"I'm every woman," Sal corrected. "Mother, Sister, Maid, Nurse." He bit his lip, thrust his hands in the dirty dishwater, and braced himself for the snotty response to come, but Randy — mute — gazed bug-eyed at the TV screen. *Don't just sit there*, Sal thought. *Fight back!*

For a moment in the flickering light, Randy looked to Sal like the college student he had seduced at a fraternity mixer ten years ago. Randy had been brimming with the promise of sex, recklessly flirtatious, cocksure. The devil-may-care glint in his eye was charming. *I wouldn't care*, Sal had thought at the time, *if he fucked me or fucked with me*. The video over, Randy shifted on the stiff sofa, and he struck Sal as diminished, a young man in his 30's with the face of a 60-year-old. His ribs stuck out from his ratty Heaven 17 t-shirt; his clavicle pronounced and gathered at the bone with loose skin. Yet when he turned to address him, Sal noticed Randy's devilish grin.

"Oh Nurse?" Randy asked, his features animated by cruelty. "Could you come fluff up your poor little AIDS patient's pillows? Pretty please?"

"I'm off duty."

Randy lobbed the pillows onto the floor. "I'm tired," he mocked. "I cook, I clean — "

"Really?" Sal hurled a fork into the sink, spattering dishwater on the wall. He stormed into the living room. He ran a finger over the television screen — static igniting at his touch — and swirled dust between his fingers. "What's this?"

Randy pushed the mute button on the remote control, pointing it at Sal.

"Look!" Sal demanded, snaking his finger across the coffee table. "Everything's filthy."

Randy glanced at Sal's smudged fingertip. He followed it as Sal pointed out where the room could stand a little cleaning, but Randy didn't see dirt.

He saw waste.

He stood up to circle the room, consider their belongings. Everything they owned was mismatched. Tie-dyed textiles that Sal made in college were draped across the corners of the room. A mahogany wet bar, given to them by the long dead owner of their favorite sex club, divided living room from dining area. A small end table sported ceramic figurines of the Jetsons cartoon characters in a nativity tableau, with George and Jane as Joseph and Mary, and Elroy as the baby Jesus. Cradling Elroy/Jesus in his palm, Randy felt disgust that someone had wasted time hand-painting these cartoon figures in day-glow oils. *Who would do something so stupid?* he thought, before remembering the afternoon he and Sal spent crafting a manger and cradle from popsicle sticks! "All this whimsy," he said, knocking Elroy from his cradle. What would his parents think?

He returned to the couch. Directly in front of him was their coffee table, a dolphin-shaped mosaic set on wrought iron legs. They'd found the table during one of their first dates; it had been too extreme not to buy, a private dare between young lovers. They carted it back to college in Sal's pickup. In a wheat field outside Moline, they took the table from the flatbed and proceeded to make love atop it. During their ferocious coupling they

5

must have dislodged a cobalt tile because, afterwards, Randy found it on the ground, put it in his pocket. He intended to glue the fragment back, but lost the tile soon after. Now he placed his hand over the glossy surface of the table, stroking the nick in the mosaic. A familiar buzz stirred his groin, yet the moment had dissipated by the time he recognized the urge as sexual. To have his own desire pass, barely perceived, filled him with dread. His dry mouth tasted of ash.

He began to shake, gasping for air.

Sal grabbed Randy's inhaler from a nearby desk. He slid on the edge of the sofa next to him, handing him the respiratory spray, all the while rubbing Randy's back over the outline of his ribcage.

Randy moaned under the touch of Sal's expert hands. *I remember this*, he thought.

Neither spoke, grateful for this moment of calm. It would leave soon enough, but they allowed their reprieve, stolen from the midst of chaos, to briefly disarm them.

"I should be doing something," Sal said.

"You are."

"Something else," he insisted.

"What else is there to do, Sal, except wait?"

Sal bore down on a muscle in Randy's shoulder. "You want to rot, fine. That's your business." He stood up, removed his apron. With one violent motion, he flung it at his lover.

"Thank you Betty Crocker," Randy said.

"Bette Davis!"

"BETTY FUCKING CROCKER!" Randy screamed, rising from the sofa, the apron tumbling from his lap.

Neither moved. They stared at the apron bunched on the floor between them.

Sal was rigid as a totem pole.

Randy, woozy and faint, wondered why their apartment was always this goddamn hot.

Sal reached out to steady him.

Randy swerved out of his grasp.

A good sign, Sal thought. *Feisty*. He forcefully grabbed Randy's forearm, his hand slipping around Randy's slender wrist.

Randy yanked his arm from Sal's grasp. "What do you want from me?" he said.

The directness of the question startled them both.

I want us to be well, Sal thought, pushing the idea away as fast as it came. A week ago, during a routine physical, his doctor — alarmed by a thick congestion in Sal's lungs — had suggested a blood test.

"For HIV," Sal had said, matter-of-factly.

"It could just be a virus," his doctor said.

"Just a virus," Sal repeated as if there was any such thing as 'just a virus' for gay men anymore. He rolled up his sleeve for the blood test, and though he shouldn't have dared to hope, that's exactly what he did. Defiantly.

When he had received the results yesterday — positive, as expected — he grew enraged, slamming his fist on the doctor's desk. His anger didn't stem from the results — a predetermined outcome, he knew — but from the temporary relief of his own denial.

Sal had not told Randy that he had taken — and failed — "the test."

Randy watched the tight muscles set in his lover's face. *He wants to control everything*, he thought. Bending down to pick up the apron on the floor between them, he lost his balance.

Sal caught him, pulled him up.

Randy giggled. *Christ, he looks great*, he thought. Sal used to do housework nude beneath the apron, his pendulous cock straining against the fabric that was now threadbare. Randy hooked a finger through the worn cotton of the apron, placed a hand on Sal's waist, and weakly pulled him closer.

"You're pathetic," Sal said, blinking back tears.

What are these tears for? Randy wondered. *Why is he crying? Is it about finally meeting my parents?* He lifted a corner of the apron to Sal's face to dab away the tears. He, himself, hadn't cried like that since the day he tested positive. He knew that Sal had seen their internist a week ago.

He dropped the apron.

Sal clutched it mid-fall before retreating to the kitchen.

Randy wanted to leave, go for a walk. He'd no idea what to say, so he distracted himself with busywork. He grew weary while attempting to gather throw pillows. He sat down with them on the floor instead. He grabbed one, fluffed it up. Puffs of dust flew out from the fabric.

Sal watched Randy grapple with his simple tasks. He wanted to help, but didn't budge. It was too easy to do everything for others, nothing for yourself. A year ago, after Randy's diagnosis, Sal decided to always remain calm, focused. Death would not scare him. Not Randy's. Not his own. Randy's fight was almost over; his own just beginning. He needed to pace himself.

Randy clutched a pillow to his chest, buried his chin into the supple down. It smelled musty, old. He knew what Sal was feeling, was thinking. He felt it in every immunodeficient cell of his body. And he knew they would never talk about his fear. When would the virus manifest into disease? How long would it last? Their time together — what little there was left — would pass with mindless chatter, gabbing about this or this, but never *that*.

At the kitchen sink, Sal washed the same fork three times. He was transfixed by Randy, cross-legged on the dusty floor, rocking to and fro while hugging a pillow, the melancholy smile of a daydreamer on his sweet, aged face. *I should help him off the floor*, he thought.

I should be by his side, Randy thought, *drying dishes.* Instead he rubbed the gap of the missing chip in the mosaic table and thought of all that was lost between them, all that had managed to survive.

Who will take care of you, he wondered, *when I'm gone?*

* * *

Barbara Manning sat in the passenger seat of the Bonneville hugging herself to stave off the chill that had settled in her bones since she and her husband left home that morning. It was unseasonably cold for Iowa in May, and even though Ben had said it would be warm in the car — "hot as a henhouse," he had promised — it wasn't. "You call this warm, Benjamin?"

"I'd call it steaming," he said, his lanky frame stiff as he drove.

"Not nearly as steaming as the pile of garbage you're feeding me."

She'd been dreading this trip for weeks. Randy hadn't been home for over a year. Since Christmas she'd suggested to her son that he visit. He was tentative, then blatantly evasive. Their last conversation was a relief to her, breezy and free like the old days. He invited them to Chicago to see a quilting exhibit. She said yes, caught up by his enthusiasm.

Barbara had mentioned the visit to a neighbor during lunch.

"Do you know what the 'quilt' is?" her friend asked, folding and unfolding a linen napkin in her lap.

Barbara lowered her voice, scanned the restaurant for familiar faces. "It's one of those artsy things." She blushed; 'artsy' was code for 'gay'. "Randy said it would be like a picnic!" She chuckled at the recollection.

Her neighbor didn't laugh. The set of her jaw was serious. "They call it the NAMES Project. It's an AIDS memorial quilt." She folded the corners of the napkin into tiny, precise triangles. "I can't believe he asked you to go."

Barbara dabbed at her clammy cheek with the back of her hand. Was Randy informing her — indirectly — that he was sick? He hadn't been to visit for so long! Did he have AIDS?

Next to her in the car, Ben — cheerier than usual — hummed his way through the Rodgers and Hammerstein catalog. He often sang to calm his nerves. Since she had not mentioned the NAMES Project to him, she wondered what had brought on his Broadway medley?

There was one answer, no other. He knew. He knew about their son and hadn't told her.

As cold as she had been before, she now grew feverish, and rested her head against the cool window. White edged the fields. Within the borderline of snow Barbara noted patches of red soil, recently tilled, sprinkled with seed. Wheat would sprout in a few months. How sick was Randy? Would he live until next fall's harvest?

"Are you okay?" Ben asked. He must have noticed her sudden pallor as he reached for her forehead to feel for temperature.

"I'd be better if you'd stop humming those damn tunes. You're not fooling anybody." She slapped his hand away.

"Then let's talk."

"About what?"

"Anything," he said. "Randy."

"What about Randy?"

"Sal told me that—"

"Sal?" Barbara snorted in derision. "You mean 'Bela Lugosi.'"

Ben gasped at the mention of their private nickname for Sal.

"'*Bela Lugosi.*'" She said it like an invocation, though she wasn't sure whether she meant to conjure Sal's image or cast it out. Either way, he was a demon. A decade's worth of photos proved it — from Randy's first days in Chicago when he sent pictures of himself alone until slowly, over time, this man, this. . .apparition appeared alongside her son. Who was he? Why was he always standing so close to her son? His long face was capped by a tuft of spiky black hair. Beneath a pale forehead, dark deep-set eyes glared out, druggy and lifeless. She disapproved before she even knew he was her son's lover.

11

Randy was all fun and frolic. 'Bela,' as she'd started to call him from the photos, appeared melancholy, heavy-spirited. Anyone could see they were mismatched — her perfect angel and that... bloodsucker.

Yet she disliked him for a more primal reason: he'd stolen her son, the once-radiant center of her universe. He was still that, nostalgically, in joyful memories that took place before she knew he was gay. But once he declared his sexuality, she felt him recede to darkness — that place where 'Bela' waited; where women were tolerated though never truly welcome. She had felt doubly cursed. She was a mother who would lose her son twice. First to the world of homosexuals — Bela's world. And finally, oh, finally...

She groaned.

"You don't even know him," Ben said, sure her moan was meant for Sal.

"And you do?"

Ben initially found Sal grotesque; thought him haughty, rude. Their contact was cursory, forced. A word here or there on holidays, on birthdays, instigated and orchestrated by Randy. But when Randy got sick, Sal told him what his own son could not. He came to know Sal as a man of reserve, of strength. When Sal answered Ben's questions with terse responses, he could hear his son in the background instructing him to lie. "Tell him I'm fine," Randy once pleaded. "And not to tell Mom." As wrong as he knew it was, that simple plea was enough for Ben to keep such a profound secret from his wife.

Ben phoned Sal twice a week. The news was often bleak, but he was grateful for Sal's honesty. He felt a growing fondness towards the elusive, protective man at the center of his son's life.

"I don't want to startle you," Sal had told Ben a few days ago, "but it's fair you know."

"He looks bad, doesn't he?" Ben asked, bracing himself for the confirmation.

"He's thin," Sal said. Ben absent-mindedly twisted a paperclip. He could hear Sal's terse breath through the phone wires. "He's having night sweats."

Ben, silent, waited for Sal to clarify.

"He had an ugly bout with pneumonia last month. Now there's thrush, and toxoplasmosis, and something else I won't attempt to pronounce."

He heard Sal shuffling through papers, looking for the name of Randy's latest illness.

"Who cares what it's called Ben. There isn't much time."

* * *

The Mannings drove the last fifty miles to Chicago in an uneasy silence, broken only when Ben turned onto Wellington Street and softly moaned, a sound Barbara interpreted as both a resignation and a signal that, though their son and Sal had been expecting their visit for years, they — excruciatingly slow in coming — had finally arrived. If Barbara had asked him, Ben would have told her that she thought too much, that he was only responding to the beauty of Lake Michigan two blocks away in the late morning sun. But she wasn't thinking of Ben at all, only of her son. Would he throw open the door and playfully demand of them, of her, "What took you so long?," a harmless question Barbara couldn't answer, even to herself, without resorting to lies.

Barbara thought the apartment complex didn't look like much, just a brick enclave with an undernourished courtyard garden full of mud where, had the recent weather been kinder, perennials should be sprouting. But there was nothing growing here: no seedlings, no vines. The empty grounds were more than simply barren. They had the desolate pallor of neglect.

Yet once she stepped inside, the stairwells and hallways were warm, inviting. Mahogany banisters spiraled to the upper landing. Floorboards, padded by worn carpets, croaked beneath the lightest step. Wall sconces held two plastic candlesticks each, their orange bulbs molded like flames. Their fake wax staffs were cracked and bent. Barbara wanted to straighten them, but ignored her impulse, staring instead down the hallway at one after the other, each coated with light dust, and each bulb dazzling with the glow of its electric stamen.

They hesitated outside the door of their son's apartment. 3G. Ben reached towards the apartment buzzer, but instead ran his fingers over the names printed in plastic laminate beneath it. Salvatore Gagliardo. Randall Manning. The label was creased and peeling at the corners. He smoothed it with his thumb. The tag's weak adhesive stuck for a second before buckling again.

"Wait a minute," Barbara said as he extended a finger towards the doorbell. "Let me put my face on." She was palming a clam-shaped compact, tapped it with her index finger. The shell opened revealing a mirror, a powder puff, and a circle of pale pink makeup. She stabbed at the compact with her applicator, loosening the cake of blush. She dabbed at her cheeks and forehead.

Ben had never seen her wear so much makeup. "Why didn't you do that in the car?"

"Hush." She saw delicate wrinkles in the magnifying compact. Ben reached for the doorbell. She swatted his hand away. "Give me a second."

"For what?" he asked.

She snapped her compact shut with authority and slid it into the pocket of her blazer. She smoothed her lapel with a few exact strokes. It had taken her nearly an hour to select an outfit that morning, obsessing over what would be appropriate. Black was too morbid. Red, confrontational. Yellow, frivolous. She settled on a neutral peach suit, bland yet not boring, with shirtwaist sleeves that exposed the elegant bearing of her wrists, and a calf-length sheath skirt that was proper but not frumpy. She wanted to dress well for her son, though Sal might think she did it to impress him. "How do I look?" she asked her husband.

"Stop fussing." He knocked on the door.

"I'm not." She twisted her pearl earrings, tugged at the edges of her jacket. The apartment door opened as she was checking the zipper of her skirt.

"That's a beautiful Chanel," Sal said, wanting to add 'Barbara,' but thought it best to address Randy's mother more formally. He looked at her for guidance. He could see that — caught off guard — she'd not quite settled on the expression she wanted to present to him. Her smile was forced. Excess foundation struggled to hide her fatigue. There was a sagginess to her skin that caught against the tight curve of her smallish mouth. Yet none of this mattered when he noticed her eyes, alert with fear and disdain and, he could only imagine, bright when she felt compassion. Randy got his green eyes from her.

"Sal," Ben said. "Nice to finally meet you."

While shaking Ben's hand, Sal looked directly in Barbara's eyes. She was sizing him up. Randy had warned him that his mother could be distant. "Ben. Mrs. Manning. Come in." He retreated into the foyer.

Ben took his wife's elbow to usher her into the apartment, but she stood firm. She'd demonized Sal for such a long time, fantasized him as a pale gothic caricature, that she was stunned by his imposing presence. He had severe cropped hair, straight along the scalp with slight curls at the edges, black with natural gray flecks at the temples. Despite his formality with her, he seemed friendly. His brown eyes were certainly inviting. His lips were as she'd always pictured them in his villainy; ample red, yes, but with a comic purse that was delicately impish and all the more dangerous. There was a hint of flush beneath his olive skin, an imperfection that came as a relief against his disarming beauty. She needed a moment to process him, get used to his height, breadth, warmth. How was it that he seemed this healthy? Surely it was a ruse.

Ben tugged at her sleeve, placed his hand in the small of her back to push her forward.

"I can walk," she said.

"Then do it."

"Come now," Sal said as he lingered beyond the threshold. He smiled and extended his hand to Barbara. "I don't bite."

"Don't believe him," Randy shouted from the living room. "He's luring you in for the kill."

Her son's soft, cajoling voice disarmed her, melted her reserve. She laughed, moving into the apartment, trying to peak around Sal to see her son. When she did, she grabbed Sal's arm. Her son was emaciated.

"Trying to steal my man, are you?" Randy put up his dukes to spar with his mother.

It hurt her to see him. So she grabbed him, hugged him close to avoid looking at him. He was shaking. He must have been cold. She rubbed her hand across his back, the way she used to burp him as a child. The apartment felt oppressively warm and Randy, wearing a large University of Illinois sweat suit, felt clammy. Fever? Cold sweat? Just nerves? Randy's banter was a mask to hide apprehension. To calm him — to distract herself — she'd play along.

"I wasn't going to steal your man," she said. "Only borrow." She glanced at Sal, who was glaring down at them. He stared at a lesion just below Randy's hairline. *Yes*, she thought, *take it in. Look at what you've done to him*. She cupped her hand over the offensive spot on Randy's neck. Sal's benevolent smile — the sadness in his gaze — astonished her. He had the reserve, the composure, of a killer.

Ben held back from the trio, patient for his turn with Randy. He shuffled his shoe against the floor, toe-to-heel in a faint rustle.

Randy heard the scuffing of Ben's loafers. "Hi, Dad."

"Hello, Son." Ben expected the weight loss, the pallid skin, maybe even the gaunt cheekbones and sunken hollows that emphasized his son's slight overbite. But not the dull core of those green eyes or the lackluster hue of his once flame red hair. These were all signs of his son's diminishment. He saw this. Then refused it. To him, Randy was the young boy in those photos on his study desk — red bangs dangling in front of his eyes, beaming at the prospect of discovering the world beyond Iowa. "You look good," Ben said.

Barbara felt Randy squirm in her arms, trying not to laugh at her husband's inane remark. "Look again, Benjamin," she said.

Laughter echoed in the foyer, none louder than her son's. She let him go and turned to her blushing husband. She hadn't meant to be insensitive, but had taken her cue from Randy and Sal, attempting to keep the day as light and irreverent as necessary.

"Where're our manners, Randy?" Sal said, aware of Ben's discomfort. "Take your folks into the living room. I'll get drinks." He moved towards the kitchen, away from the general unease, but called back to them, always the good host. "Make yourselves at home."

Barbara sat by her son on the rigid black sofa in a living room she could only describe — with forced generosity — as weird. *Too modern, too angular, too sterile*, she thought, as opposed to the practical, homey normality of the rest of the apartment. *Sal must have decorated this room*, she decided. Randy had her impeccable taste.

She took his hand between hers, rubbing it, content for the moment to be able to touch him. He turned away from her as she smoothed his fingers — one by one —

with her palm. His visits home had grown infrequent over the years. She had always blamed this on Sal, but in seeing Randy she had to acknowledge that it was shame that had kept him away. There were questions — basic, primal — that she wanted to ask him. When was Sal first unfaithful? When did he tell you? How did you let this happen? He'd be evasive with her, she knew that; deflect her questions with a playful change of subject. Her love for her son was strong, though their relationship had grown superficial since he told her he was gay. She'd let it happen by avoiding any discussion of his life with Sal. Yet as he sat next to her with his eyes closed, lost in thought, she wanted to know everything. "What are you thinking, honey?" she asked, stroking his hair.

Randy opened his eyes, smiling. There was an eager tilt to her head, anticipating his answer. But what would she want to hear? He was happy they were here, glad they'd come to see the place he called home, to meet the man who shared his comfort and, right, now his pain. Yet his thoughts were of Sal — *with* him — and his mother wouldn't want to know that. He said nothing.

Barbara sought out her husband, who was walking around the living room, looking at the vast array of strange objects scattered throughout it. He squinted at a popsicle-stick manger peopled with cartoon characters. His customary cheerfulness had abandoned him.

"Sit down, Benjamin."

"I've been sitting for hours."

She looked towards the kitchen where Sal was preparing iced tea. What was taking so long? Was it possible that he was being considerate, giving them time to be alone as a family? That was the least he could do! She looked at her men — Ben and Randy — one wandering around the room like a nomad, the other barely moving beside her. "I'm going to help with the drinks," she said.

Sal was scouring the stovetop. Barbara was surprised to find he hadn't fixed anything to drink, though there were four empty glasses, upside down, on the drainer.

"Finishing chores," he explained, sensing her confusion. "What can I get you, Mrs. Manning?"

She spotted a professional cappuccino maker on the counter. "Does that thing work?"

"You need something strong I'd imagine," Sal said. "Double espresso, coming up."

His mastery of the kitchen astonished her. This was his comfort zone. Clean, proportioned, well organized. He switched on the cappuccino maker, packed the filter, placed two clear shot glasses under the drip, got an elegant white cup and saucer from the cabinets above him, fished a lemon from a baggie, halved it, quartered it, peeled it, poured the frothy black shots into the bone china, and circled the rim with lemon rind before dropping it, with a twist, into the espresso. He handed her the coffee.

"Anything else, Mrs. Manning?"

She scanned the mug in her hand. For what, she wasn't sure. She knew well enough that the disease wasn't born on the air or in a coffee cup. Still she examined it for any telltale traces, until she saw Sal staring at her. "Yes," she said to him. "Call me Barbara." When she noticed that her son and husband had left the living room, she added, "I've been abandoned by my men."

"I can see that."

"It seems we both have." She lifted the cup to her lips, winking at Sal as she tasted his bitter espresso.

Randy and his father were in Randy and Sal's bedroom where Ben stood at the foot of his son's bed. Randy rifled through a sock drawer.

There was a red wooden toy-box near Ben, the one he'd made for his son when Randy was five-years-old. It was where Randy kept his playthings: a fire engine, board games, a G.I. Joe. Ben bet it was still filled with his son's old toys. He propped up the lid with his foot and saw a thick black dildo, a ribbed vibrator, a clutch of red balls on a string.

"Here we go," Randy said, pulling an envelope from the drawer. He turned as his father slammed the lid of the box. "I'm still using it to store all my unused toys."

Ben blushed. "What'cha got there?" he asked.

"This," Randy said, loosening the red twine clasp, sliding papers from the mailer, "is the Last Will and Testament blah blah blah." Ben sat slack-jawed. "And you're the executor."

Ben stuttered. "I'd be honored, Rand, I would, honestly. But what about Sal?"

"He's done enough already." Randy was thinking of the future, after his own death, when Sal would face the signs of his body's betrayal. A cold that becomes pneumonia. A sinus infection that turns into shingles. Nausea. Blindness. Dementia. He handed his father the envelope. They sat side-by-side, shoulder-to-shoulder, at the foot of Randy's bed, reviewing instructions. Sal would get most of Randy's possessions. He'd left a few items for his parents, including the toy box. (*Though hopefully not*, Ben thought, *its contents*). There were instructions for Randy's burial in the Iowa family plot. Explicitly, and most importantly as it was underlined twice in red marker: when the time came, Sal would be buried next to him. "You have to promise me this, Dad."

Ben wasn't certain he could get his wife to go along with this. But that didn't stop his reassurances. "We wouldn't have it any other way."

With a little help from Barbara, Sal prepared a bland lunch — slices of kiwi and mango, watercress salad.

"I'm used to eating like this," he said, "so Randy doesn't feel like he's missing anything."

Barbara peeled the overripe fruit. Sal made Randy a macrobiotic shake. She watched him as he poured the thick goo from the blender. "Does he like this gunk?"

"Can't stand it."

"Then why?"

"Cleansing elements," he explained. "Easy on the colon. Something like that."

"Has it helped?"

"Does it look like it?" He said this as gently as possible, but he could hear the distress in his voice. "I'm sorry."

You should be sorry, she thought. If her son and Sal met in 1978, had been together for over ten years, the only way they could have been exposed to the AIDS virus is if they'd been unfaithful, if Sal had been—how else to put it?—fucking around. He was older than Randy by a few years; he'd be more likely to — what did they call it in her day — 'step out.' She ran her hands under the running faucet, her fingertips covered by the sticky juice of the kiwis. "I have no right to ask this, Sal, but—"

"Why Randy, not me?"

"If you'd been faithful, none of this would've happened."

He could only smile as she blamed him. He was not surprised. He'd anticipated it. Still, she'd no right to be so smug. He could explain to her that he and Randy had been devoted to each other. They'd been tender and constant, loving and companionable. Doting, even. But faithful?

No.

On occasion, they dabbled in combinations of three, that magic gay number. But Randy — how they laughed at the accuracy of his name — picked up men in bookstores, bathhouses, parking lots, anywhere. Sal — a few years older — was less compulsive, yet understood the need.

"Faithful?" he said to Barbara. "In a way, yes." He gathered the pile of fruit rinds on the counter and threw them in the sink, compacting them into the disposal.

She hadn't intended to offend him. She placed a hand on his shoulder.

"Don't," he said, flicking the disposal switch. The drain gurgled like air caught in the back of a throat. The cloying perfume of pulverizing rind lingered in the air.

She should have stepped away, attended to the business of lunch — setting the table, filling glasses with ice — but she persisted. "I just don't understand. You've been together since before this — this — the H.I.V. thing started."

"Mrs. Manning."

"Barbara."

"Mrs. Manning." He clicked off the disposal. "Your son is everything to me." His voice was barely audible. *"Everything."*

She leaned towards him to hear what he was saying.

"I can't bear his suffering," he continued. "If I could die first, give you more time with him, I'd do it."

"That's not what I mean."

"But it's what you want. Why shouldn't you? I respect that. But this thing, Mrs. Manning; this is no one's fault."

She couldn't help but admire his smooth restraint, his discreet denial. It was clear to her — as he refused to lay blame — that he was protecting himself, his culpability. She gathered slices of fruit from the cutting board, arranged them in a china bowl Sal had placed out for such a purpose. Didn't he just think of everything! She couldn't bear him. "Don't treat me with kid gloves," she said. "I need to know if—"

"If I'm sick? No. Not yet."

"But—?" She was dizzy with confusion.

"The H.I.V.?" he said, escalating the sounds of each letter like a question. He tilted his head, indicating to her that he was considering his answer, weighing it, but he was just looking into her hard eyes trying to determine if she might have one flicker of compassion for him. "Yes," he said. "I have the H.I.V."

How was it possible? she wondered. There was one answer — one answer only — that she could keep at bay, and briefly at that, by phrasing it as a question.

"From my son?"

24

Patchwork

Part One; Chapter Two

RANDY STROLLED THE neighborhood with his mother; happy she was in Chicago, pleased to be with her. He tilted his head slightly to feel the cool breeze on his face, relieved to be out of that stuffy apartment. As he walked, he swung a Marshall Field's shopping bag at his side.

"Good days are few now," he said to his mother.

"The summer will be here soon," she said.

He wasn't sure if she misunderstood him, or was gently guiding their conversation to neutral ground. "Summer," he said back to her, "followed by autumn, followed by winter, followed by. . ."

Barbara slapped his forearm. She wanted to bask in whatever small pleasures her son had to offer, not wallow in morbidity. As they approached the car, she decided on a seating arrangement so that she could spend more intimate time with him.

"Why don't we have our—" she began, but stumbled on the exact word to use to refer to Ben and Sal, who followed closely behind them. *Husbands, companions, lovers?*

"Men," Randy offered. "Our men."

She nodded her head.

Sal, arriving at the Bonneville first, held the rear door open for her.

"Our *men* can sit up front," Barbara said, "since Daddy's driving the car and Sal is directing-" Sal grabbed her above the elbow to aid her into the car, flustering her. She associated the gesture with her husband's vigilant consideration. "Daddy's driving and Sal is-"

"Waiting for you to get in," Randy said.

"Yes," Barbara said, and to Sal, "such a gentleman!"

The back seat was cavernous. Too short to reach the floor, her scrawny legs dangled in the Bonneville. She flexed her feet, and the round scuffed tips of her shoes scraped across the gray floor mat.

"What are you doing, Mom?" Randy asked as he slid into the car, tossing his shopping bag between them.

"Getting comfy, Son."

Randy felt cramped, anxious in cars, even one as spacious and solid as a Bonneville. He preferred walking, a luxury he'd taken for granted until he was too weak to make it to the local record store three blocks south to buy a B-52's single for Sal.

Ben revved the engine while pulling cautiously out of the parking space. "Are you ready to cruise?" he asked.

"Always," Sal said wryly, glancing back to see if Randy was smiling.

Randy fidgeted. Having just left a controlled environment, he didn't want to be in another, more confining one. He preoccupied himself with small bits of business. Rummaging through his shopping bag, he placed a swatch of fabric and a Sony Walkman on his lap. He tossed homemade cassettes to the seat, the plastic casings cracking as they fell.

He noticed everything. Compressed heat blew from the vents. The motor purred. His father turned right on

26

Broadway. There was backup from road construction, orange pylons as far as Randy could see. Cars funneled into a one-lane merge. He cracked the window for fresh air. Viscous tar stench flooded in. In the oncoming lane, impatient motorists honked, racing from church to catch a ball game, tires whooshing on wet asphalt. Things moved fast and slow outside the shell of the dark green sedan, though Randy — content for life to wash over him again, if only for a moment — folded and quartered and smoothed the fabric resting in his lap: a patchwork piece he'd made, in his own memory, for the AIDS quilt.

"What'cha got there?" Barbara asked, fingering a swatch.

"It's a blanket," he said, smoothing the quilt where his mother had touched it, "in case I get cold."

She knew he was lying. Even folded, the fabric was too thin to generate sufficient warmth. What was he going to do with it, toss it around his shoulders like a mink stole?

"Is that for the AIDS thingy?"

"*The AIDS thingy*," Randy spat out, glaring at her, repeating the phrase harshly until she grasped how ridiculous she sounded.

"I don't know what to call it," she said, blushing. "If you had told me sooner I would have *brushed up* on the lingo."

"Well go on, *girlfriend*," he said, slathering his voice effeminately. He clicked his fingers twice with a limp-wristed fling.

"Oh, snap!" Sal exclaimed to himself.

In the rearview mirror, Ben saw Barbara's mouth drop open. "Okay back there?" he asked.

She couldn't meet her husband's gaze as he spied at her in the mirror, nor at Sal who kept glancing edgily into the backseat. Mostly, though, she couldn't look at her son. She'd wanted him to banter with her, tease her in that way that suggested everything was fine, but with respect, as Mother to Son. She tapped her toes on the floor mat.

"How hard is it to remember, Mom?" Randy said gently, aware that he had gone too far. He could see it in the blush of her cheeks. She was embarrassed. But of herself or him? The tapping of her foot ceased. Stone still, he knew she felt trapped, an animal in a corner poised for a moment to strike back. He wouldn't give her the chance. He was enraged by her willed silence, her conscious ignorance.

"Once again," he said, "it's called the NAMES Project Memorial Quilt. For P.W.A.'s. That's *People with AIDS*. The ones who are rotting in their graves, and the ones who are rotting on their feet, like me."

"Don't," Ben said, barely a whisper, yet enough to silence Randy.

Randy glanced at his father, at the back of his gray head of hair, and then quickly out the window, shamed. He'd always been able to prod, and argue with, and anger his mother for no other reason except that she could take it. But his gentle father, whom Randy always found unerringly sensitive and magnanimous and kind: to hurt him — even indirectly — was unbearable.

They drove on, the car's nascent internal silence discomforting. Ben suppressed the urge to hum. Barbara flicked lint from the lapel of her suit. Sal stared intently at buildings he'd ignored for years on his daily walk to work at Billy Bud's, the shop he owned and built into the premiere brand of avant-garde floral design in Chicago's gay enclave. He neglected pointing it out as they passed by, not from forgetfulness or modesty or even the crippling disinterest that overcame him whenever he had to explain to anyone what it was that he did for a living, no. It was much simpler. He didn't want to see the shade of either hidden disappointment or smug unsurprise on Barbara's face when she was told her son's lover was — imagine that — a limp-wristed *florist*. Yet more importantly, he hated the fucking place. In the last half decade his business had tripled, but for every bouquet that went out the door for a wedding or the birth of a newborn, *five* gorgeous, architectural, inventive cornucopias that impressed the high-class homos and stank too sweetly of death were delivered for funeral after funeral after motherfucking funeral.

Randy rubbed the plaid upholstery of the back seat. His father had bought a new Bonneville every three years since 1962. Though the ride was smoother with advances in engineering, the seat fabric got pricklier with each model. Over time the cushions—heavy blends of canvas and polyester—ensnared odors between their bulky layers. And though the car was new and the air inside it still carried a hint of the manufacturer's factory-floor freshness, Randy thought he could smell or detect or remember, in the bulging lumps of compressed foam, the muggy scent of October rain, the stink of high school sex. When he had just turned 15 in that stifling month of Indian summer, in a car remarkably like this one — he took his first cock. He was amazed at his precise knowledge of it; his responsiveness arrived at genetically, complete and encoded. Leaning over that boy — *what was his name?* — taking him into his mouth, he was thrilled though not surprised by the flesh's metallic taste, the way that smooth red cranium pulsed against his tongue, its fat green under-vein snaking from base to head like the Mississippi on a Braille map. It was easy, so second-nature that Randy knew, in the instant it took to tell his brain to quell his gag reflex, that he'd been born to suck cock.

Only afterwards, when the favor had been reciprocated, did he feel the guilt, which came as suddenly as the impulse to sleep. He felt what he'd done was as natural as breathing, though he also knew — for the time being — to keep it secret. When he slipped into the house after midnight, Barbara rustled from the sofa where she'd waited for him.

"Where've you been, young man?"

"Practice," he said, smiling sheepishly at a truth he hoped she'd misinterpret as studying on a school night.

She flipped a light on in the hallway and scrutinized him, as she always did, for signs of problematic behavior: cigarette smoking, drug use, the standard adolescent traumas, but in his paranoia all he could think was: *This is it. She knows.*

His mother grabbed his hand. "What did you do to your knuckles?"

He had banged them raw against the car window when he came earlier.

"I dunno," he shrugged.

"You kids!"

She came close to him for a kiss. The boy's taste was in his mouth — nicotine, Schnapps, cum. Would she detect the sharp tang of semen on his breath?

He turned his head.

She grazed his cheek, lingering a moment longer than necessary. Ruffling his hair, she sent him upstairs. "Off to bed, knucklehead."

"Okey doke," Randy said aloud, the first words anyone had spoken in the car in the last few minutes.

Barbara, startled, reached out and touched Randy on the shoulder. "What's that, honey?"

Randy looked at the person on the seat next to him. He wondered whose car he was in. He saw Sal in the front craning his neck to look at him. The reflection of his father's eyes, full of confusion, flashed in the rearview.

"Okey doke," he repeated. "Just talking to myself."

"Don't want to talk with your old Moms and Pops?" Ben asked.

"And say what?" Randy picked up the Walkman from his lap, cradled it in his palm. He inserted headphones into his ear and pretended to depress the silver play button, staring out the window, ignoring his father.

"Let him be, Benjamin," he heard his mother say. She touched his hands, running her fingers over his knuckles.

Randy noted the crack in her voice, her sad gaze towards him. As she massaged his hands—the same ones he had callused all those years ago, the only evidence at the time of what he'd done, of who he *was*—he thought again of his night with that boy, his name lost forever yet his taste close as the brine on the air, and was certain that his mother had known, had *always* known. There'd never been any need to tell her.

31

He approached his illness in the same manner. He knew they'd figure it out from his absences, his refusal to visit them at home. He knew they would say nothing, not from lack of care, as he once thought, but out of consideration. They'd waited, *respectfully*, for him to come to them. He hadn't; he couldn't. Sal did. How could Randy tell them, tell *her*, how sorry he was, that to let them know he was sick was to admit to himself that he was going to die?

"Thank you," he said, and his mother stopped rubbing his fingers, taking this as a cue to let go of his hand.

He pushed 'Play' on the Walkman. Leader tape spooled around the playback heads. Music clamored, picked up tempo. A guided fury of sounds took him back. He nodded with every sharp snap of the snare drum, fixed in the rhythmic grasp of a fierce nostalgia.

He used to drink and cruise, flirt and fuck, with extravagant abandon. He was beautifully seductive, had soft red bangs, flush skin, seasonal freckles. His wide lively eyes and artless smile gave him the deceitful appearance of a country rube longing for corruption. Innocence primed for defiling — was anything more sensual? Well, he was certainly spoiled now. His body, once an instrument of liberty, was now a trap. He longed to return to a time when he could feel, not merely remember, desire.

*   *   *

Metro passed on the left—a new wave palace abundant with neon and a blinding, dizzying disco ball. The place was ridiculous, but Randy had gone once in 1983 at the urging of Megan, his friend. When was the last time he'd thought about her?

The sight of the club brought her back to him in full regalia.

Megan, shaped like a Bartlett pear, had dressed her bulk in layers of cascading white—stockings, bodysuit, taffeta, lace. She wore opera-length gloves with cutout fingertips; smoked clove cigarettes from a long white filter. Though overweight, she was pretty beneath her pasty make-up, caked silver eye shadow, and pencil-thin eyebrows. She wore slick black hair in a bowl cut which she tied back with a white silk headband. All this, a natural birthmark on her left cheek, and her failed marriage to a college sweetheart whom everyone — his parents included — knew was gay, completed her eerie resemblance to a bloated, booze-addled Liza Minnelli. Megan was a world-class fag hag. The only reason no one had ever called her that to her face was because everyone mistook her for a drag queen.

Near midnight, the Metro DJ deep-scratched a funk riff. Synthesized scat wailed from the speakers. *Ba um ba um ba um bop bop*. Bass rumble lifted Randy's red bangs from his forehead.

"I love this song!" Megan had squealed as she grabbed Randy's arm. She parted the writhing throngs by force as she took her rightful place dead center on the dance floor. Exhausted, Randy wanted to sit the song out, but her enthusiasm, coupled with a powerful clutch, won him over.

Positioned directly beneath a mirror ball, Megan had an uncanny ability to know just when it would rotate, throwing shafts of sharp light like a cage around her, and she spun — always — in the opposite direction. If anyone encroached her twirl space, or got too close to Randy, whom she not-so-secretly loved, she'd swing out her arms, pretending not to notice as her fist slammed into unsuspecting flesh. Her irrational jealousy flattered Randy, though he had always been clear with her that he would never fuck her.

Instead, they went dancing, often, as on this night, where she twirled and dipped and swooshed, all her unspent sexual energy informing her moves. Randy swayed, pacing himself, mouth dry. Sinister vocals penetrated the air. A robotic voice sang about the pleasures of dressing every day as if it was Halloween, and Randy thought the song couldn't be more apt. He was surrounded by people in costume: an amyl nitrate popping swashbuckler; a lanky nerd in a yellow jumpsuit with a red clay flowerpot on his head; an underage suburban debutante slumming in a black corset, the baby fat of her back pushing through the tight crisscross of her bindings.

Diana Ross, or a reasonable facsimile, approached him. "I'll let you fuck me if you got a big dick."

"It's a surprise package," Randy said. "Besides, it's not the meat, it's-"

"Honey, please. More meat is more motion." Was Randy's hearing damaged by the loud music, or did Miss Ross have a slight lisp? She fluttered her long fake eyelashes at him, curling back her puffy blue-black lips in a smile that revealed a set of alarmingly crooked teeth. Wrapping an arm around Randy's neck, she pulled him close, the sage tranny about to impart queenly wisdom.

Randy mimed a yawn.

"There are two types of people in this bar, child," she told him. "Size queens and liars. And, baby, I ain't gonna spread for no lies."

Loving a dare, Randy had unzipped his fly. Miss Ross reached in, rummaging through the slit in his underwear. She gave his sweaty dick a sharp yank, smiling or laughing, he couldn't be sure. He felt hot and woozy, probably the blood rushing from his head to his prick. He saw Megan twirling fiercely, her fist balled tight, then heard a piercing smack as she landed a hard right on Miss Ross's strapless left shoulder. The drag queen's grip loosened, ripping her hand from Randy's pants to bitchslap Megan, hard, once on each cheek.

"Don't you *evah* touch me again," she snapped, before appraising the pitiful sight before her. Her tone softened, and she leaned towards Megan. "Listen, *sistah*. That Liza drag is tired." Reaching into her rhinestone clutch, she pulled out a business card and slipped it between the knuckles of Megan's still-balled fist. *Transformations, for the Modern Wo-Man* the card read. "Call me. We'll get you a whole new look."

How could anyone mistake Megan for a drag queen? Tears streaked her mascara and pancake make-up. She caught a glimpse of herself in mirrors that lined the walls of Metro, the severe hair, broad shoulders, puffy folds of white trailing to the floor. She sought out Randy, her damp black eyes more needy than ever.

Randy started to laugh—she looked like a drenched mime—then stopped. He felt compassion for her, so much sympathy he was sick. Could you feel a friend's pain to such an extent? He grabbed Megan's shoulder, gave her a squeeze to assure her she'd be all right, and passed out on the floor.

Megan had known before Randy did that he had AIDS. He'd suspected that night at Metro, but told himself a series of lies. He was dehydrated. His body was changing with age. He had an iron deficiency, needed exercise, should start taking B complex vitamins.

"All this denial, Randy! You sound like me," Megan said. "I'm as much at risk as you are. How many closet cases did *I* fuck?" She took his hand in hers, gently stroked it. "Let's get tested. No matter what the results, we'll be there for each other."

"Drama queen," Randy said. She seemed painfully sincere at the time, but when her test came back negative and his positive — "Always a trendsetter," she quipped — he learned the true depths of her performance. She didn't completely withdraw, but she stopped coming to the apartment. All contact they had was by phone.

"I'm *so* busy lately," she said the last time he spoke with her. "What with grad school and work and Tommy — oh, he's divine, Randy. I can't wait for you to meet him. Maybe this weekend."

He knew she would never come to see him. Randy was grateful when his gay friends stopped visiting, extricks that couldn't bear to see the future he represented: their future. When they came to call, he couldn't stop wondering if he'd infected them. They were thinking it, too. There was incrimination behind their blank looks and polite conversation. Yet Megan's retreat felt like a betrayal. Was their friendship that insignificant to her?

"Come by on Saturday," he said, pressing her for an exact time.

"I can't, Randy, I-"

"Why not?"

"Tommy and I are driving to Wisconsin to-"

"It's not an airborne disease, Megan."

"I know, it's just-"

"I won't make you as *sick* as you're making me right now."

"It's not you, Randy. It's me. I can't handle it. Everybody I know is dying."

"*I'm not everybody.*" Randy waited for her to respond, to tell him that she loved him, she'd try to find the courage to visit, their friendship meant that much to her, but all he heard was breathing. Shallow breathing.

"Gotta go," he said.

"See you soon."

"No you won't."

His favorite club didn't have a name, just a number, 7-5-1, as nondescript as its industrial decor. Hidden in the cellar of a brick two-story, 7-5-1 was encased by Chicago's L tracks and black steel girders. From a distance, the club looked trapped beneath a giant metal spider web. He'd been there many times before noticing its name was its street address. Disappointed, he took to calling the club 13, the sum of its numbers.

The last time he'd gone, September 1981, had been a Tuesday night after work at the American Bar Association, a job of paralyzing tedium exacting membership fees from paranoid young lawyers who clung to their money like it was the last ounce of coke in their wallet. He needed to blow off steam, dance a little.

The crowd at 13 was sparse when he arrived. Megan was supposed to meet him at 8:00 p.m. He drank lager and played darts while he waited. The music, English and gloomy, droned in the background like a dentist's drill. The new punks, the "post-punks" as they were called — on the dole in dead-end industrial towns — sought comfort in doomed romance. When love failed they howled, in minor chords, from its bloody grave-yards. Joy Division was Randy's favorite band, not for their songs, which were relentlessly depressing, but for their following. Suburban boys in leather pants and crisp white tees accessorized their boredom with an angst as loving and calculated as a Beale Street drag queen.

Tuesdays at 13 were *Love Will Tear Us Apart* night, named after Joy Division's most popular tune. Around 9:00 p.m. the suburbanites poured in, fresh-faced lads in butch drag with their studied scowls. Soon they sur-rounded Randy, and he quickly forgot how angry he was that Megan, still nowhere in sight, had stood him up.

(Had this been the night, this September night, when he got infected? The endless possibilities muddled any certainty — nor did he insist on knowing — yet this en-counter, romanticized in memory, held vivid in his mind. If he had to endure the indignities of his body shutting down, at least let its inception resonate.)

One of the gloomier songs ended, so despondent it barely had the energy to fade. The brush of high-hats blared from boxy floor-level speakers. Randy made his way to the center of the dance floor, breaking through the line of clubbers stomping in unison. Simple chords surged from the din. Randy grinned and thrashed, free-form, body unfettered by the limits of standard dance. The beat, high and bass heavy, echoed through the cavernous room. Lighting was dim, but a strobe-lit survey of the faces around him confirmed that, at 27, he was older than anyone else in the bar, and the only person smiling. Music, even with such grim purpose, made him giddy. He squealed, his delight not overlooked by the solemn faces around him.

His laughter, taken as a sign of disrespect for the music, was his ploy to get the young roughs closer to him. One by one they circled him, pogoing, shadowboxing, spritzing him with the sweat that shook from their close-cropped hair. This wasn't dancing. This was foreplay. Randy jumped up, buoyant in the air, shimmying his shoulders. He thrust his neck like a preening bird and cackled, pissing them off even more. They boxed him into a smaller space, a circle for slam dancing. A young man crashed against his chest, toppling Randy into a massive swell of bodies. Randy sprung at him. The kid tumbled backwards, caught his balance then lunged. His fist pounded the air. The other hand latched onto Randy's crotch.

Randy was no longer the only man on the dance floor smiling.

"Take me back to your place," the kid said.

"What about your friends?" Randy asked, surprised that he'd be so indiscreet in front of them.

"What friends?" He was on the short side, compact, blonde fuzz covering his scalp, eyes slate blue. His grin was lopsided. He wore silver dog tags, one wedged in the hard cut of his chest. One hand was thrust in his pocket, clutching his dick. He put his free hand on Randy's hip. "What do you say? Wanna go?"

"You ask a lot of questions," Randy said, teasing him as he stroked the damp hair at the back of his neck. "I have a lover at home."

"I'll fuck him, too."

"You're not his type. What about your place?"

"Can't. I live in Skokie."

"Too bad for you," Randy said.

"With my parents."

"Even worse." Randy rolled his eyes and walked away.

The kid grabbed him by the neck. His grip was forceful; his hands cold and damp.

"Outside," he demanded.

Randy thought for a second. *September, still warm out. Why not?* "Yes, sir."

"Rolf," he said, flashing him the name on his dog tags.

"So it says," Randy said, derisively. His name was most likely Brent or Jasper, a clean-cut sophomore studying political science who dressed in skinhead drag because it made him look fucking hot. Randy couldn't stop himself from licking his lips.

Under the L tracks behind 13, Randy had squatted in front of Rolf. The pouch of his leather pants was cracked and stank of semen. Rolf grabbed a handful of Randy's fine red hair, grinding his crotch against his face.

"Play nice," Randy said.

"Bite me, bitch," he said, and giggled.

Randy unzipped Rolf's pants. His cock tumbled out. Randy caught it on his tongue and guided it into his open mouth. As he went down on him, Randy undid his own jeans and slid them past his knees.

Rolf moaned. "Your ass is so fine," he said.

Randy stood up, lifted his shirt over his head, and turned his back to Rolf. He looked over his shoulder at him and drawled in a thick Southern accent. "Don't you want to fuck me? Ain't never had it in the butt before."

Rolf pushed into him, not as rough as Randy hoped, but confidently, with precise slow strokes, pressing him against the brick wall. Music vibrated from the club. Cold dog tags slapped against Randy's back. He pinched and twisted his own nipples. After a minute his legs went numb, knees trembled. He leaned into Rolf, reached back to grab his scalp. "Bite my neck," he said. "Bear down."

Rolf pulled out, spit on his cock for more lubrication, hovered, teasing, then thrust, swaying his hips from side to side. Randy moaned, softly at first, murmurs that escalated to the howl of Rolf's name.

A woman leaned out of an apartment window. "Shut that fucking dog up."

Rolf took off his army tags, shoved them in Randy's mouth. They tasted metallic and salty, just like Rolf's semen. Randy came without touching himself. The pressure in his ass, the sharp grab of his sphincter on Rolf's cock, forced his orgasm.

The L train sped overhead. Sparks shot from the steel wheels of the braking cars. Rolf pulled out, moaning, sore. Randy sighed and checked his watch. 1:57, exactly. He could never understand why he remembered the digital glow of those numbers. 1:57. 7-5-1. 13. They were simple numbers, with fixed values, forced into significance by combinations of fate.

Randy's legs were shaking. As he splayed against the wall, he had felt the pulsing vibrations from the music inside the club. "Meet me inside, whoever you are," he said, "and buy me a beer before last call."

* * *

Randy pressed the rewind button with the tape still in play mode. Music shrieked in reverse. He started the tape again. A slow drum roll erupts into muted chords – a punk fanfare – before a dissonant thrash crescendos in a headlong tumble of chanted shrieks. The sound of fury marshaled and pointed; rage polished to its knife's-edge gleam. An impassioned song, like a great fuck, can startle you into clarity. Punk – wasn't that the music to soundtrack the end of days? Though, in retrospect, it wasn't the end of days at all; just the beginning of them.

Rolf had been his real name. An obituary appeared in the *Chicago Tribune* a few months back with a small headshot of a beaming teen next to two inches of copy. Rolf Jansen, 1963-1988, only child of Klaus and Birgette, Father an international banker, Mother on the board of several children's charities. Their son recently passed the Illinois State Bar, practicing copyright law.

The same night he'd read the obituary, Randy, who thought he had flipped on a public access station, watched a silver-haired Southern Baptist inform his television parish that they could not hide their abominations. "There is *no* such thing as anonymous sex," he said, pointing a finger that, over the years, grew permanently crooked with blame. "God has marked *those* people. *Everyone* will be known in the end."

Who had Randy marked? Whom had he infected? Who had he hurt, betrayed, abandoned, isolated? Wasn't it enough to know he'd brought this to bear on Sal and his parents?

The song repeated. Randy hadn't remembered taping it twice in a row! He lowered the volume on the Walkman. He opened the car window all the way, stuck his head into the breeze. The sting of brisk lake air colored his cheeks. It was cooler than when they left the apartment. His mother shivered, but said nothing about the open window. *She'll never complain*, he thought, *only persevere*.

"Over there," Sal pointed, the Sears Tower visible in the middle distance.

"A marvel," Ben said flatly.

"Ooooh," Barbara agreed, the slight raise in her inflection suggesting otherwise.

Randy could tell they were humoring Sal. Treading lightly, peacekeeping.

Had Randy asked his parents here to hurt them, ignore them? He'd been a selfish man, a selfish son. They were kind to him. He was distant. How he wanted them to know him! Could they? What would they be willing to do? If not embrace, at least understand? His frenzy for sex was never about love or experience or pleasure — those were incidental. The bedrooms, the bookstores, the bathhouses, the back rooms — they were only about one thing.

More.

He snapped off the Walkman.

There was a tap on his knee. The car had stopped. His mother had unclasped her safety belt.

"We're here," she said.

Ben smiled at him in the rearview mirror.

Sal, who had opened the car door for Barbara, walked around the trunk and stood near Randy, fingers grasping the door handle.

"I'll be right there," Randy told them.

He gazed down the stone walkway leading to Lake Michigan. Along Navy Pier were other families. Some accompanied their dying children; others had come to memorialize those who were gone. They strolled toward the exhibition hall at the tip of the pier. Randy's parents, with Sal at their heels, fell in line behind them. He put his Walkman on the seat next to him. The quilt piece, still on his lap, warmed his legs. He picked it up, rubbing the thin fabric against his cheek before tossing it in his shopping bag. Down the walkway, he saw his mother look back first to see if he was following, then his father checked, and finally Sal. He gestured to each one in turn that it was okay to go on, go on ahead without him.

Patchwork

Part One; Chapter Three

ONCE HE CAUGHT up with them, Randy walked along Navy Pier flanked by his parents.

Sal kept a respectful pace a few steps behind, noticing — in the distance — a crowd lingering outside the entrance.

There'd been rain that morning though the day was bright and clear now, with dampness riding the sharp lake breeze. Wind in Chicago was never soft, Randy thought, but angular, with power to slice through the heaviest clothes. Though he was wearing jeans, a sweatshirt, a pale blue windbreaker zipped to the neck, he knew his mother was worried that he wasn't warm enough. She kept tugging up the jacket zipper as if he was five and she was dressing him for a snow day. "Are you trying to snap my head off at the neck?" he said.

Barbara placed her cold hand on his warm face. She rubbed her thumb against his dry cheek as if brushing away a tear. This unexpected gesture — so intimate — embarrassed him.

"Mom!" he said, blushing.

"Mom!" she repeated, smoothing the shiny jacket folds against his chest to flatten the air pockets, sealing in the warm air.

"We'll be inside in a minute," Sal said. As they neared the Exposition Hall, he saw two separate groups — those standing behind a velvet exhibition rope, and those, cordoned off by a police barricade, carrying placards with quotes from scripture.

Ben wondered if his wife, susceptible to colds, might want to borrow his plaid wool scarf to wrap around her throat. He removed the muffler and handed it to her.

Sal and Randy emitted low moans of disdain at the ugly, old-fashioned material.

Barbara held the scarf at arms-length to study it. "I'm not wearing this," she said. "It doesn't go with my suit."

"But it's cold," Ben said.

"When hell freezes over, and then only maybe, will I wear this *thing*." The scarf rippled in the breeze. Barbara tossed it back to her husband.

Sal and Randy nodded agreement with her decision.

And then a voice, deep and resonant, rose above the gathered crowds.

"'God, take pity on me! Cure me, cure me, for I am impure.'"

"If it isn't the welcoming committee to hell," Sal noted.

Ben tried to give the scarf back to Barbara. "You'll need this now."

"My enemies say, 'How long before you die and perish?'"

Randy searched the protestors to find the speaker, but couldn't match the words to a face. Too many mouths were moving at once. People in line moved slowly towards the entrance, talking quietly in pairs, staring at the ground to avoid eye contact with the crowd twenty feet away. To Randy, the silence of the patrons felt like a confession of guilt. How could they listen to such drivel and not say anything?

"I deserve my misery, they reckon. I do. I deserve it. I want more!"

"Go on, girl," yelled a young black man. He twirled his wrist and, punctuating his point, snapped his elegant fingers.

"What girl?" Ben said.

"Sickness, fatal sickness, has overtaken me," said the still anonymous speaker. *"I'm going down, always going down — not for the first time, but for the last."*

A small crowd exited the hall; the line slowly moved. Barbara wrapped her hand around Ben's arm. Randy, a hand on Sal's shoulder, followed his parents towards the opening, still scanning faces behind the barricade. They were as he expected — white women, a few years younger than his mother, dressed in Sunday polyesters. A few young men wore dark suits and starched shirts. They clutched Bibles embossed with gold lettering. The converted listened to the words being spoken, nodding agreement or smiling with benevolence. Randy had no patience for conformity — religious, political, sexual — and he had a dirty urge to dismiss the Christians with a 'fuck you.'

"'Pity me! Raise me up, oh lord, and let me enjoy, oh let me enjoy, your favors.'"

"Get a life!" someone shouted.

"Get an afterlife," yelled the speaker.

Randy saw him, a man roughly his own age. He was hunched from atrophy, curled inside a rented wheelchair. Lesions dotted his throat like a necklace.

"Sinner!" he cried, the voice surprisingly strong. He singled Randy out with the stab of a short hooked finger for punctuation. As he pointed, a black wool cloak fell from his shoulders. "God will take care of you."

47

How could Randy explain that God, the idea of Him, held no comfort? When his own pain grew unbearable he would turn not to religion, but morphine.

The man shook in his wheelchair, his finger scratching at the rubber armrest. He tried to pull his cloak back up around his shoulders, but had trouble clenching his hand around the material.

Sal saw the alarm on Randy's face. He stepped out of line, past his lover, moving towards the barricade. He bit his lower lip, afraid he would explode with anger at this stranger's incriminations. Yet as he reached the wheelchair, ready to put this sanctimonious fool in his place, he felt Randy's hand on his forearm, indicating restraint.

There was an innocent grin on the man's ravaged face. Randy wondered if he had been handsome once? It was hard to tell behind the scars on his cheeks and forehead. Yet his smile was inviting, masking frustration as the man bashed the steel wheelchair girders with the meat of his raw open palms. Randy studied him as the man stared past Sal, and briefly at Randy, then beyond him still: at the tarnished black girders of the pier, at the Lake Michigan shoreline to the east. There was peace in his smile, serenity in his dementia. He kept banging on his wheelchair — neither rhythmically, to Randy's ear, nor randomly. The longer he listened, the more Randy believed that the drumming was a type of code, a *communiqué*.

"*He*," the young man shrieked, his eyes wild with compassion, "*He is everywhere. Don't you kn, kn, know,*" he stuttered, his teeth chattering. "*Don't you kn, know Him? His love, in a biblical sense, will keep you warm.*"

Randy couldn't watch the man shiver any longer. He reached over him in the wheelchair, grabbing the black wool cloak. He draped the loose material over the young man's shoulders, wrapped his neck against the wind, tucking the slack between his shoulder blades and seat-rest.

"There now," Randy said, patting the wool against his body, "it's almost over."

"*No, no,*" he said, "*it's just beginning.*" The young man cackled, gazing at the skies. A sharp ray of sunlight pierced his eye, but he didn't blink, didn't flinch. The man was blind.

* * *

None of them had expected the vastness of the NAMES Project quilt — certainly not Ben or Barbara, who knew next to nothing about it; not Sal, who'd heard of it in passing; but especially not Randy, who hadn't thought it would fill the cavernous enclave of the Exposition Hall. They stood at the precipice of the exhibit; four figures that from a distance appeared dwarfed by the encroaching reams of material laid out before them.

Upon entering the space, Randy shielded his eyes to the harsh light, as interrogating as in a surgical theater, the type of shadow-less radiance he imagined as the fabled glow of the afterlife. Randy didn't believe in the concept, but in case he was wrong, he'd rather go to hell, where soft flickering flame would illuminate him best.

He adjusted to the heat — Exposition Hall was humid, an atmosphere where spores thrive — with open-mouthed breaths. Was it lake brine he tasted on the dank air? He scraped his tongue across his upper teeth to get rid of the flavor, a combination of rank algae and chlorine. Had he given it more consideration, he would have known it was just the aftertaste of his macrobiotic lunch, but Randy was preoccupied with the AIDS quilt before him, and the panel that he held against his chest.

He had become fascinated by the NAMES Project since he saw an article in the *Chicago Reader* a year ago when he was ill with pneumonia and bored by bed-rest. Sal has been working constantly to support them and help pay the medical bills. He hadn't wanted to burden his parents with visiting. His friends had died, abandoned him, or both. He admired P.W.A.'s, People With AIDS, who demonstrated against everything from governmental testing policies to pricing practices of pharmaceutical conglomerates, but felt no community with them. Making a quilt — while not as glamorous as saving the world — gave him focus. Each spare healthy minute he had he devoted to crafting his panel. While he might no longer be able to walk, his patch would roam cities he'd never visit, his name spoken by sweet lips he'd never have the chance to kiss. Now near the end of his life, he searched for the ideal spot in the quilt to launch his new journey.

The quilt covered the floor space from wall to wall, long and wide as a football field. Patches, roughly four by three feet, were displayed in sixes, clusters bordered by two inches of red cloth, with walking space on the chalky concrete between each group.

The first piece Sal noticed was a stark white quadrangle with black embroidery. *Martin*, no surname. *1954-1983*. *29 years old*, he thought. "Such a proper name," he remarked to no one in particular. He said it twice: "Martin. Martin." There was a nostalgic quality to the name, as if conjuring the image of a clean-cut young man of a long-ago time, another age. As he gazed upon the acre of patches still before him he thought, *yes, exactly, they are all names from a passing era.*

Barbara trailed onto the jagged pathway behind her son and Sal. "Oh, my," she said, stepping lightly, careful not to tread the edges of the fabrics below her. She was as considerate of the panels as she would be with gravestones in a cemetery. Browsing the clusters quickly, her eye retained a name here, *Elsie*, and a small, often comical detail, like the tiny decal of a cow dotting the 'i' in her name. Another patch featured a faded Polaroid of a burly chef, *FrankieLoveMuffins*, twirling the edges of a thick mustache caked with flour. Many panels were like lighthearted, gentle moments relished and retold, but Barbara could feel no joy as she looked out at the hundreds of pieces she had yet to see. At first, the quilt seemed soothing, a pleasant checkerboard of colors and memories, but as she walked closer to the center of the floor, where there was no escape from the loss each patch signified, the assault of patterns turned dizzying.

She shut her eyes, hard, and shivered. Was it her mother who told her as a little girl that a sudden chill was the result of a ghost passing through the body of the living? Her mother told her all sorts of nonsense, wives tales. She never knew when to believe her. Barbara shuddered again. Could her mother have been right? There were too many ghosts in this room. She needed a solitary moment to collect herself.

"Barbara."

Had a woman's gentle voice called her name? Perhaps she'd said her own name silently, as a mantra, a word to clear all thought from her head, but she would not be left alone. There was the sound of a throat clearing, and Barbara's name was spoken again, with the faint trailing of echolalia. *Barbara, arbra, bara, ara, a.* Other names followed — *"Cyrus Jackson. Little Johnny"* — all resounding throughout the hall. She opened her eyes to find the source of the words. Ben was, as always, at her side. Randy and Sal stood a few yards in front of them, huddled closely, gazing down at the floor.

In the far left corner of the hall, a woman at a podium, clapboard in hand, softly recited the names of the dead.

"Would you look at that?" Ben said. Barbara thought he was talking about their son and Sal holding hands, but Ben hadn't noticed them. He crouched down to get a closer look at the panel by his feet, a canvas ghetto landscape finger-painted in oils and signed by the artist, *Jefferson*. There was a row of brown tenements with big silver trashcans at the bottom of each set of stairs. A red fire hydrant squirted a thick stream of white water. Stick people of all colors stood on stoops. In the upper right corner, a brilliant sun shot squiggly yellow rays over the top of the buildings. Dates were stenciled onto the canvas in black ink, probably not by the artist. *1980-1987*. Six years old.

"This is like those valentine's cards kids used to make in kindergarten," Ben said. "You know — the square house, the curly hedges, me and you on the lawn with our pink cheeks and big goofy smiles. Randy always drew me with buck teeth."

Ben touched the rough, crusted paints on the panel and sighed. "'Love you with all my heart,' he wrote, with a red heart instead of the word. Remember those cards, honey?"

"You've got them up in the rec room. I see them every day, Ben."

"It's the damnedest thing," Ben said, gazing up at his wife, then over at his son. "I can't stop thinking about him as a child."

"He's a grown man," she said, watching Randy and Sal wander in the midst of the quilt, hand in hand, stopping now to scrutinize another patch, shoulders touching, heads tilted slightly towards each other, their bodies in perfect compliment. Barbara had wondered if an outward display of affection between her son and Sal would bother her. It did, but not in the way she expected. When Sal, upset by a cluster of panels, stepped awkwardly back from the quilt, and Randy reached out to balance him then stroke his cheek with his thumb, Barbara found the gesture not only intimate but agonizing.

Sal wouldn't let go of Randy's hand. They strolled the walkways, appraising the panels together. One patch for a drag queen sported long curled eyelashes and vividly gaudy eye shadows that made them laugh. Sal was delighted by the imagination in all of the patches, the common materials chosen by each of the survivors to best memorialize their loved ones. The selvage on a stockbroker's quilt resembled tickertape. A dancer had the steel tips of tap shoes around each side of his name like quotation marks. Sal found an aspect to admire in every piece, regardless of whether the patch was stitched (and glued and ironed and stapled) by the hand of a novice, or lovingly detailed by an accomplished quilt-maker. When he spotted the panel for *Matteo*, in three strips of color for the Italian flag, he felt the power of the quilt over his own memory.

Randy, recognizing it as the name of Sal's estranged father, immediately slipped his arm around Sal's waist to hug him.

"I feel so foolish," Sal said.

"About what?"

"I haven't seen my father for twenty years. Haven't thought about him in ages." He made a sweeping gesture with his arm. "Then there's his name and it all comes rushing up."

Ben escorted Barbara down the walkway toward Sal and Randy, joining them in front of Matteo's panel. They scanned the fabric: the Italian flag, an outline of the country sketched over it, and a black silk star sewn on the Tuscan coast.

"My father was born in Viareggio," Sal said, leaning down to touch the star. He looked up at the Mannings. "My mother died when I was 12. He threw me out when I was 16."

Without thinking, Barbara asked "Why?" She knew the answer and, blushing, turned from him.

Sal knew the question was innocent, but he was angry she hadn't controlled her curiosity. He waited for the further invasion of privacy he now expected from her, but she said nothing, instead looking to her husband to lessen her embarrassment. Ben smiled absent-mindedly, his fingers nervously tapping out a song on his pant leg. Sal turned to Randy — the only family he had, all he felt he'd truly needed. They shared a quick, bittersweet smile. Sal saw Ben, benign and anxious, and Barbara, blank and impenetrable. Did they know how lucky they were to be at each other's side after forty-odd years? Growing old with your lover had become a privilege. Did they feel grateful to be with their son, ailing as he was? Did they have even a touch of pride over the fact that they hadn't abandoned him out of prejudice?

*   *   *

Tiring as it was, Randy was determined to see all the patches on display in the Chicago exhibition. After a thorough tour, he'd yet to decide where to put his patch. He circled back to the center of the quilt, followed by his parents and Sal, and noticed a piece heavy with text, a poem by Rilke. He knelt to the ground to read the elegant letters, one column in German, the other one its English translation. A line struck him.

"*Tote sind beschäftigt,*" he read aloud.

"What's that?" Barbara asked.

"'*The dead have their own tasks.*'"

"And I was so looking forward to a vacation," Sal said, mock disappointment in his voice.

"This is the place," Randy said.

"For what?" Barbara asked.

"The unveiling," Randy said, unfolding his panel and relishing the drama. He smoothed the creases in the fabric with his wrist, snapped a few strands of frayed thread between his fingernails. The patch was rough, stitched by an amateur. He'd used a faded, chestnut hand-me-down quilt from his grandmother as the foundation, and had cut, with pruning shears, thin ribbons of purple, red, yellow, green, blue, and orange, the colors of the rainbow flag. The lengths of strips varied, torn in places and shredded at the edges, sewn with loose stitches that buckled the fabric and gave the flag the illusion of waving. He spelled his name in black felt save for a loud pink triangle representing the letter "a."

R▲ndy.

He leaned back to see how his piece fit among the other panels. "Kind of obvious, sure," he said. "Too much symbolism." He flicked a piece of white thread from his jacket. "Oh well."

Barbara gasped, placed a hand at her throat. She could feel a headache coming on.

Ben, dumbfounded, could manage no words, only short, shallow breaths.

"That's quite—," Sal started, laughing instead at the hideous panel. He had to look away. Why hadn't Randy asked him for help? He could have smoothed away the rough edges, taught him to stitch with more confidence.

Barbara kept staring at the panel and the garish rainbow flag in its middle, that blatant celebration of homosexuality, before her eye was drawn to the fabric that embedded it, culled from an old blanket given to Barbara by her mother before she died.

"It's called the Swallow's Nest," her mother had told her, spinning another loony folk tale. "See the pattern raised here, dearie, like four swallows, tails touching in a circle, here, beaks pointed there, towards the future?

During the Gold Rush, when a Mother covered her son with this quilt, he would awake full of wanderlust."

Barbara had never listened to what she thought of as her mother's bullshit. She ignored her, kept her at arm's length, left home the day she turned 18. When she visited her mother, which was infrequently, she'd interact with her the way she might an acquaintance. Here was her son, stooped over a clump of tawdry fabric, and she knew she'd also made him into a stranger. *The dead have their own tasks* he'd said not a moment earlier. A chill passed through her. She started to tear, silently at first, until her sadness manifested in faint, steady whimpers. Finally, breathless, she opened her mouth to sob.

"Are you all right, Mom?" Randy asked. He heard her sighs, and tried to make visual contact with her, but she had covered her eyes.

"I'm fine," she lied, searching her palm for traces of running makeup. "Thank God for waterproof mascara."

Randy had a little plastic case with sewing materials in his jacket pocket. He removed a needle from it, previously threaded, and knelt down to next to the quilt. He unfurled the patch he had created, smoothed it at the edges, and began to sew the panel into the quilt.

Ben, shell-shocked and ashen, stared at Randy. Was his son always this thoughtless? He felt ashamed, not by his wife's ongoing tears, or the small crowd that had gathered near Randy's patch while pretending not to notice, but by his son's effrontery. He grabbed Randy's arms, pulled him up, stunned by the virtual weightlessness of his son's body.

"Look at me, goddamn it," he said. He searched Randy's eyes for a glint of understanding. "How could you think we'd forget you?"

"I didn't think-"

"No, you didn't, about anything but yourself." Ben wanted to shake his son, smack some sense into him, put a little luster on his pallid cheeks, hold him, protect him, and stop him from shivering. There was so much rage in him he didn't know where to direct it. If he could locate the source of Randy's goddamn disease, he was certain he could crush it single-handedly.

Randy winced beneath Ben's tightening clutch, but didn't move from it. His father's harsh words were more painful than his grasp, though the pressure Ben put on his biceps forced him to drop the spool of thread, the needle trailing it to the floor, rolling towards the patch which had been crumbled up in their scuffle.

Alarmed, Sal leaned forward and grabbed Ben by the wrist. "You're hurting him."

"It's OK," Randy said to Sal. "I deserve it."

Ben released his son. What could he mean? What did he deserve? Hadn't he been through enough, more than Ben could ever imagine? He felt petty, raging at his son. He embraced him, cupped his head in his hand and ran his fingers through his thinning hair. He kissed him on the cheek then rested his head on his shoulder, inhaling deeply, breathing him in. Randy smelled of antiseptic soap and, beneath it, a cucumber moisturizer, the kind his wife would use. *Let me remember*, Ben thought, *the scent of my child's skin*.

"I know, Dad," Randy whispered in his father's ear, stroking Ben's back, but what could Randy know of how Ben felt?

Ben didn't want to let out the sweet breath it would take to speak. And to say what? He'd never been shy about telling his son he loved him, Randy knew that, but to tell him what was in his heart, that would be an act of bravery. "All these patches, these memories," he said, pausing, his mind racing from what he'd started to say towards what he needed to say. "You can't begin to *imagine* what it will be like to lose you."

*   *   *

Sal knelt on the floor by Randy's panel, smoothing it out. The patchwork before him was unrefined, the idea of it injudicious, but Sal admired Randy's enterprise, full of that loopy spontaneity that had attracted him all those years ago. The rough fibers of the rainbow flag reminding him of the auburn hair on Randy's chest. His thumb grazed the raised pattern of the foundation quilt, smooth and delicate, like the touch of Randy's calf resting on his shoulder when they made love. And the itchy felt in the letters of Randy's name!

He could feel the Mannings close behind him, their warmth. Though he could sense that what he was doing was calming to them, he wanted this moment alone.

"Randy, I'll be done with this in a minute. Why don't you take your folks outside for some fresh air?"

"Just one more look," Randy said, lingering a moment before sidling between his parents and walking them towards the exit.

Sal straightened the patch, aligned it beneath the red selvage surrounding the other panels. Though he hadn't sewn anything for years, Sal picked up needle and thread. He stitched, loosely at first, until his strokes gained control. When he reached the end of the panel, he double-stitched a tight knot, kneeling against the cold floor to bite off the loose strand.

He stuck the needle into the spool, put it into his pocket. Standing, he stared down at the patch. The more he contemplated it, the less imperfect it became. Unfinished, maybe, petulant even, but attractive in its way, like a quiet boy not yet confident of his own impenetrable beauty. What detail, Sal wondered, would complete this patch? What could Sal attach to it that Randy overlooked?

He started to walk away, chuckling at the ragtag thing he'd just sewn against the others. Randy's actions may have been misguided, foolish even, but Sal also found it oddly beguiling.

He turned to look at the patch from a distance. There it was amidst its new community of strangers and fellow travelers, one of hundreds, no more or less compelling than any of the others. Such fierce individuality! Such comforting anonymity! These contradicting ideas nagged at Sal as he distractedly smiled at the solitude of Randy's name at the bottom of the quilt.

For all his maverick spirit, Randy never could bear to be alone.

Sal checked his pockets for a pen, intending to write his name beneath his lover's, when he pricked himself with the needle in the spool of thread. A drop of blood appeared on his thumb. Hastening to the panel, he knelt down and pinched his thumb to quicken the flow. He pressed his thumb to the quilt three times. The deep red prints formed across the fabric. He stood up and stepped back too quickly, a bit woozy but determined and steadfast. He read, aloud.

"Randy. . .", the name trailed by a bloody ellipsis.

Patchwork
Part One; Chapter Four

THOUGH SAL DIDN'T expect him to make it through the 80's, Randy held on, determined — it seemed to Sal — to usher in one more decade. As the year ended and the 90's began, Randy suffered a bout of dementia from which he never fully recovered. On that New Year's Eve, Sal uncorked a bottle of champagne and let the bubbling overflow trickle across Randy's lips.

"You made it," he said, rubbing the liquor into Randy's mouth with his thumb. "Welcome to another fucking decade."

For six weeks, Randy floated in and out of consciousness. Before dawn on the morning of Valentine's Day, snowflakes from another winter storm melted against the bedroom window that overlooked the apartment courtyard. Dabbing sweat from Randy's forehead with a damp washcloth, Sal glanced over at the west wing of the building. Three apartment windows, diagonally from the third floor right to the first floor left, were lighted like the grid of a tic-tac-toe board.

The rest of the building sat dark.

"What do you think?" Sal asked, pointing towards the window. He talked to fill up space in the room, to diminish the echo of Randy's asthmatic wheeze. Those sibilant breaths with their viscous throaty resonance sounded much like, yes, Sal had to admit, a death rattle.

"Who will wake up next?" he asked. "Mrs. Moska-vitch or the Lumley's?"

He thought he saw Randy's foot move beneath the blanket, big toe pointing towards the window.

"Right," Sal said, then spoke like a game show con-testant, enthusiastic but with a shade of desperation. "I'll take Mrs. Moskavitch to block, Gene."

Randy snorted in agreement. For days, he'd commu-nicated with grunts, twitches, the lolling of his rheumy eyes to the left or right. Sal was amazed by how effort-lessly he understood every sound and move he made.

Another apartment, not Mrs. Moskavitch's, lit up on the first floor. Sal could see the blue flicker of flame beneath a red teakettle on an olive green stove. The vi-brant tints against the dark dawn astonished him at first, though they quickly dulled, as did everything else these days, until he was no longer sure what colors he had seen, and was left with only the sad surprise that he had noticed them at all.

Blankets rustled. Randy grabbed at Sal's hand — he wanted him to remove the washcloth from his forehead. His grip was weak yet urgent; his breathing phlegmatic. Sal knew he should check on him. Still, he couldn't turn away from the window.

He will be dead, Sal thought, *in the time it takes for that kettle to boil.*

Bright florescent kitchen lights came on in another apartment.

"Sal," Randy said, his voice cracked, feint.

"I know," Sal said, disappointed that they'd picked the wrong apartment in their private game of tic-tac-toe. He turned to reassure him. "We should always go with Paul Lynde for the block."

He brushed thin strands of matted hair from his lover's forehead. Whatever strands remained clustered at the edge of his hairline. Sal believed Randy had willed these last few hairs into bangs. He pressed the back of his cool hand against a feverish cheek, ran a thumbnail across parched lips.

Randy gasped for air. His head dropped to the right. *To look out the window*, Sal thought. He immediately stiffened his neck and gazed up at Sal. His once luminous eyes had grown murky. For a moment in the predawn light, they seemed clear. A delicate smile formed about his lips.

Sal looked away, scanning the apartments for the red kettle, the blue flame. He couldn't locate it and turned back to the bed.

Randy's beatific smile disappeared. He took his last breath with ease, as if after all this time he suddenly recalled how effortless it could be to breathe in, to exhale. Everything about him seemed relaxed, welcoming. His eyes, for a moment, sparkled with what Sal thought could only be desire.

"Oh Sal," he said, his body easing further into the well-worn mattress. "*Fuck me.*"

* * *

Snow continued to fall as Sal called number after number from a checklist he'd compiled prior to Randy's death. He dialed EMS to have Randy's body taken to the morgue. He called a funeral parlor in Chicago to arrange for an in-town memorial service, another in Iowa for the burial. The outpatient hospice would need to make arrangements to remove the web of medical equipment that flanked the bed. *Their bed,* he started to think, though he hadn't slept in it for months.

Five hours passed as he struck names from the list. Friends made over the last few months called — out-care nurses, delivery guys from the Angel Food meal service — each offering Sal genuine condolences and numbers — so many different numbers! — for "grief counseling". He checked his watch. 10:43 a.m.

There was one entry left on his list. He had scribbled Randy's parents down as "Mr. & Mrs. Manning", underlined twice in black marker. Their placement at the bottom of the list had been deliberate. He didn't want to bother them with the details of funeral arrangements. If he needed it, he would have time to compose himself for the call. As he dialed the phone, he knew there would be no sufficient amount of time to prepare to tell a parent that their child had died.

"Ben here," Randy's father answered, cheery as usual. As soon as he heard Sal's voice, he dropped the phone.

In the background, Sal heard him mutter *"Oh God,"* but anything after that was muffled by the phone being retrieved and a hand cradling the transmitter. Before she got on the phone, he could hear Mrs. Manning tell her husband to hush.

"Hello, Sal," Barbara said. He could tell she was distracted by Ben's cries in the background.

"Mrs. Manning," he said. Before she could correct him, he addressed her by her first name. "Barbara."

He heard her breathing — shallow, gradually deepening as she composed herself, setting her jaw for the day ahead. He imagined Ben at the kitchen table, head bowed, his wife standing behind him, one hand on his neck, the other clutching the receiver. He'd never been in the Manning's home, but envisioned a round oak table in a breakfast alcove, the phone, bright yellow, mounted on the wall. There must be fruit ripening on the windowsill, even in February.

Did he hear Barbara rustling through a drawer? What was she looking for? A pencil? A Valium for Ben? A checklist not unlike his own? He smiled, suppressing a giggle that, though inappropriate, he needed. He expected her to ask for the details of her son's death, the time, last words, everything he could remember.

Instead she asked, in the kindest voice, "What can I do to help you?"

He felt guilty as he told her, "There's nothing left to do."

. . .

Barbara knew Sal was wrong. There was plenty to do. For a start, Ben had to be sedated. After the doctor came to administer the shot, Barbara tucked her husband into bed with minimal fuss, wrapping him from neck to foot like a child in a papoose.

She spoke briefly with distant relatives. Against her better judgment, but out of propriety, she informed the neighbors — asked them graciously — to respect their privacy until the funeral. She didn't want a bombardment of folksy gift bushels full of gingham-wrapped canning jars — "grief baskets" she called them; jams and fruit preserves better suited to a bed-and-breakfast than a funeral.

She gathered herself, went about her normal business. Bills had to be mailed. There was laundry to wash, vacuuming to be done, dusting, organizing. Barbara attacked her chores militaristically.

By mid-afternoon, the house was spotless. She poured herself a double-bourbon. Though she drank infrequently, she did it fiercely, given to hard proof alcohol that lined their bar. The bottle was drained by early evening. She passed out in the family room; woke after dawn the next morning.

She checked on her husband. He was snoring, a dollop of drool upon his cheek. How could she wake him? He would see the day, remember death, and sob all over again. Best to let him sleep.

The coffee she made she swallowed without tasting. She leaned against the kitchen countertop, tapping her chipped nails on the Formica. A manicure before the funeral would be necessary. What else was there to do today? Make coffee — done. Serve Ben breakfast on a TV-tray — not today. Do the crossword in the morning paper, yes.

The paper must surely have been delivered already. She opened the front door. The porch was full of cast-iron pots stuffed with baked beans, baked chicken wrapped in foil, chocolate cakes in airtight Tupperware containers. As asked, the neighbors had respected their privacy. They must have quietly placed food on the porch before backing away, careful not to disturb them in their grief.

Maybe they had tried to ring the doorbell then peaked through the bay window blinds to catch her passed out, an empty bottle of Crown Royal at her feet. It hardly mattered. The trail of dishes that lead to their door was a sign to any passersby that death had come to this house.

She looked for the *Waterloo/Cedar Falls Courier*, didn't see it wedged beneath a serving tray. She moved the neatly prepared foods from the porch to the kitchen. *Who's going to eat all this?* she thought. Not the grieving, who slaked their appetites on booze and Percodan. Not her son, who would never savor the aftertaste of cloves in a wedge of cured ham. *Who then?* she wondered, scraping perishables into plastic bags to freeze for later use.

* * *

The snow that had begun the morning of Randy's death continued to fall four days later, only now it seemed to Sal that it landed in thick sheets on the streets outside the apartment. Wind rattled the thin apartment windows. Mornings and afternoons were indistinguishable from dusk. That fourth evening, Sal moved aimlessly from room to room. Catching sight of himself in a full-length mirror, his lanky figure wrapped in a flannel blanket, he said to himself, "Oh, if it isn't the ghost of L.L. Bean."

Heaters clanked and hissed, hot to the touch, yet outside their warm immediate radii the rooms were drafty. With no other body to absorb the impact of sound and heat and air, the space Sal inhabited was cavernous.

He cracked the blinds open with two fingers. "Enough with the snow," he said, his voice reverberating throughout the living room. Its echo comforted him until the echo was gone.

Randy's body had been shipped to Iowa yesterday. The funeral was in the morning, but Sal would not be leaving Chicago. Planes had been grounded at Midway and O'Hare. The bus station was closed until further notice. L trains were running, but not to Iowa.

Trapped inside, he was not alone. Randy haunted the apartment. Everything he had held, brushed against, sat in or slept on, danced around or fucked with. There was the smell of his hair on a tortoise-shell comb. The cleft in the mattress where he lay dying for his final months. Fingerprints inside a jar of flour. Randy didn't need to manifest as a ghost. He'd never left their apartment.

His presence wrapped around Sal, python-esque, suffocating him. To break free, Sal would have to sell everything — the business, the furniture — and move. He could thrive only if he lived his life for the future, whatever future this disease had in store for him. After grief, nostalgia could kill him.

"Randy," Sal said, as if his lover were standing at his side. He pulled the blanket tighter around his body.

* * *

The cemetery was on a small patch of hillside in an otherwise flat stretch of town. Driving toward it in slow procession, Ben noticed clustering headstones of various sizes and craftsmanship. Sun hit the stones so brightly Ben could not read the graveside markers. He opened the automatic window of the limousine to let air into the stuffy compartment.

"Why is it that it's so warm here and Chicago is buried under snow?" he asked Barbara.

She leaned forward. She was wearing a black suit accentuated by a black hat with a rim that looked to Ben like the rings of Saturn. Warm as it was, there was a chill in the car. She hugged her arms against her chest, rubbing her elbows with her fingers.

"You think Sal could have made it here," Ben complained.

"Don't be foolish," Barbara said, dismissing her husband. "I'm sure he tried." She caught a glimpse of herself in the smoky limousine partition. There was lipstick smudged along the corner of her mouth. She removed one white glove to fix the tiny imperfection with her pinkie. "Facts are facts," she said, referring to the snowstorm in Chicago. "Besides, we grieve in our own ways."

Ben conceded: facts *are* facts, yes. His wife's every action denied the memory of their son. She cleaned, organized, listed. She spent hours at the beauty parlor. And today! She didn't just look good, he thought, she was turned out for a performance.

The limo stopped. Ben, always the gentlemen, walked to Barbara's side of the car, opening the door for her. As he extended his hand to her, he asked, "How is it, exactly, that *you* grieve, Barbara?"

She stared out from under that heavy black rim, her eyes shadowed so that Ben could not see her hurt and surprise. She smiled at him, gently slipped her gloved hand into his palm. Outside the car she touched his shoulder, but when she tried to look at him, at the anger and confusion on his face, she found herself gazing beyond him, at the casket and the flowers and the small crowd of mourners in gradations of black.

"I grieve," she told Ben, "quietly."

"You grieve," he said, "secretly."

He turned from his wife and walked towards the grave. The scarlet casket refracted the morning sun. He thought of Sal, how heartsick he must be regardless of where he was, then of Randy, how lucky he was to know such tenderness and concern, and finally of his wife walking behind him, picture perfect as the anguished Mother.

There was a tug on his jacket before Barbara placed her gloved hand on his shoulder, a wife reaching to her husband for support while they moved towards the grave of their only son. She held a pristine white handkerchief in her hand and dabbed at her eyes beneath the dark veil, eyes that, Ben noticed, were decidedly dry. There were sniffles coming from the crowd gathered at the gravesite. The slimmest smile played across his wife's dour lips. He reached up to touch her hand resting on his right shoulder, rubbed her fingers a second, entwining them with his, and lifted her palm from his body. It seemed he would hold hands with her, side by side; instead, he gently guided her arm to her side to let it rest alone before taking the tiniest sidestep away. Starting to cry, he thrust his hands into his jacket pockets, fingering his handkerchief there. He would not wipe the tears from his face. There would only be more.

Barbara, who couldn't have planned his breakdown better, blotted her husband's wet eyes with her handkerchief before touching the damp material to her cheeks. The moisture that settled there stung as if she had cried tears of her own.

*   *   *

The night of Randy's funeral, Sal — in bundles of thermal clothing, his face wrapped in a gray kaffieyeh that exposed only the narrow slit of his eyes — trudged south on Halsted toward the nearest gay bar, a brownstone duplex with the unfortunate name of "Mother's." He had visions that he'd be greeted by a matronly English gentleman with a ridiculous overbite who called everybody 'ducky.'

"Howdy, pardner," the bartender shouted above the hot throb of Detroit house music as Sal entered.

"Hey," Sal said, barely audible. Except for the two of them, the place was empty. There were pinball machines flashing and bleeping in the corner. The bar opened onto a dimly lit sitting room of velvet salmon couches. A spiral staircase, its copper railing rusted green, lead to a second floor, but Sal didn't know what was there. A piano bar? A dance floor?

"What can I getcha?" The barman was upon Sal before he'd had a chance to unravel his many protective layers of clothing.

"Something hot," Sal said, folding his coat onto a barstool.

"I can definitely supply that."

"Brandy," Sal said before the bartender went on. He unraveled the black wool scarf, draping it imperviously around his neck like a boa. "Slow night?"

Without responding, the barman placed a snifter at Sal's fingertips.

"This is half-empty," Sal said, flicking the rim of the glass with his fingernail. He was surprised when it chimed as only real crystal could. "*Chin chin,*" he said, raising the glass. The first pull stung as he swallowed. The second soothed his throat. The third settled warmly in his stomach.

As soon as the stem hit the counter, the barman refilled the snifter to the rim. He handed the glass to Sal, spilling a bit on his own hand. "*Chin chin,*" the bartender said, licking brandy from his palm in a slow, sensual circle.

This seemed to Sal such a blatant come on that he didn't mind being a bit forward himself. He sat on his barstool, sidesaddle, and leaned his upper body over the bar to get a fuller look at the barman.

He was about five eleven, with an enticing though overeager smile. He had on leather chaps — in winter! Beneath them were jeans worn white at the crotch. His denim shirt was open to the waist, exposing a nipple ring with a heart charm resting against his shaved chest. He had light eyes beneath a white Stetson that made him look young. The wrinkles at his temples suggested otherwise.

Those pale eyes — were they hazel? blue? — twinkled in the flash of light from the nearby pinball machines.

"How you doing there, pardner?" the barman asked. To Sal's ears, he had a slight accent. Maybe it was the word 'pardner' and its easy slip into redneck caricature; maybe it was that laconic Memphis drawl Sal could hear him trying desperately to veil. Either way, Sal felt no need to answer the barman. He pointed at the glass that still held a knuckle of brandy.

"Just let me know what you need," the bartender said. "I can fill you up all night."

Sal rolled his eyes and the bartender shrugged. Was he simply over-friendly on this dead night, or did he want Sal? He certainly was attentive! This boy — his enthusiasm made him seem no older than 22 — was of an average beauty, nothing special in a high-density area of homos, yet, Sal thought, probably a knockout in Tennessee. His eagerness could just as easily be read as impatience — he never stopped moving. Sal watched him pace, full of surplus energy, stalking the length of the bar as if there were other patrons. His strides were long; the space behind the bar was roomy. At each end he pivoted on the ball of his foot like a professional dancer. His compact body, admirable as it was, just made him another in a long line of gym clones. He was a tired cliché — a dime a dozen.

The only aspect of the bartender that really interested Sal was the color of his eyes. As the barman moved, passing through various densities of light, his eyes changed color — cold blue in the glow of the streetlights, hazel from the strobe of the pinball, dark — dark and wet — in those instances when he was in shadow. What might they look like where the light was steady, when the boy was pinned beneath him, staring in his eyes with desire, audacity, astonishment?

He sat at the bar until closing, drinking moderately. After 2a.m., he followed the bartender to his studio apartment a few blocks away. They'd not exchanged names; there'd be no point to it. Sal imagined that years from now neither would be able to describe a single detail about the other.

Yet as he undressed the bartender in the tight space of his studio — discovering the individual shapes and flavors of this new body — he found the man might be harder to forget. He removed the hat from the man's head, revealing tufts of fiery red hair. He pulled the bartender closer, parting his lips for their first kiss. His spit tasted vaguely familiar, antiseptic from the mouth-wash he must have gargled in the bathroom at the bar just before they left. Later, as Sal fucked him — safely, of course, having slipped on that greasy sheath of prophy-lactic impersonality — small details accumulated until he had no choice but to notice the freakish similarities to Randy: the bowed legs, the bent cock, the flat fuzzy ass, that goddamned mouthwash that wasn't minty or fruity or masked with fake flavors, but rough, astringent, raw.

Sal clamped his eyes shut, concentrating on this mo-ment, this boy, this room that smelled of garlic oil and Irish Spring. Yet stroke after stroke brought Randy back. Ferocious rhythms. Voracious contractions. The arc of the bartender's spine, his full hips, the grind backwards onto Sal's thick straining cock. Even the way he moaned was comparable — a sharp whine of discomfort that es-calated into a sustained howl.

Sal thrust deeper, the condom tight at the base of his dick, his pubic hair caught in the prophylactic's rim. When he came — the barman on his back now, swaying from side to side as Sal fucked him furiously — he pushed his cockhead firmly against the bartender's prostate so he would feel every clench and flare of Sal's orgasm, exactly the way Randy liked it.

The only difference was that when the bartender came, he stopped the sway of his body and looked down at his dick giddily, astonished at the full stream flying from his prick as if the fluid now gushing was a startling,

unexpected conclusion, as if it had never happened before. He kept his eyes open — wide, wider, nearly pulsing with his orgasm — their sparkle and clarity disquiet-
ing, their color light yet distinct from Randy's — warmer,
more awestruck, less guarded.

But Sal was too busy fucking the image of his dead
lover to notice.

Patchwork
Part One; Chapter Five

SIX WEEKS AFTER Randy's funeral Sal drove to Waterloo in a rental van that stank of sour milk and lurched forward when downshifting. A snug baseball cap tilted slightly to the left over his forehead. He felt it suitable for the operator of a large piece of machinery — even a reeking van — to not only wear headgear, but to sport it at an angle.

As he drove, he fingered the felt rim of his hat as a *'howdy'* to all the motorists he passed by, especially the truckers, those fat cocked burlymen made legend in Joe Gage's grainy 70's pre-condom porn classic *Kansas City Trucking Company*. What was it about driving that kept Sal's dick semi-hard? Was it the aimless liberty? The promise of a clandestine rest-stop encounter that lurked around every corner? The temporary denial that here he was, pushing 40, jobless by choice, HIV positive, strangely optimistic while staring down a future he could only imagine as blank.

He knew he'd be dead inside five years, yet he felt unbound, buoyant.

Arriving at the Manning's, a modest farmhouse nestled amidst the gaudy sprawl of modern estates, he took off his hat, first to the memory of his lover, then to the reserve of his lover's childhood home. Switching off the ignition, he crawled into the rear of the humid van where he was flanked by the remainder of Randy's possessions. He was grateful to have had them; relieved to be rid of them.

"Let's get to it," he said, addressing the piles of things. He'd visit a while with the Mannings, not too short to be impolite, but not too long to be tedious. He'd no intention of telling them he was leaving the Midwest, or where he was going.

He wasn't sure himself.

The oppressive heat in the van wasn't helped by the fact that Sal was clad, head to toe, in black. Workboots, jeans, turtleneck, baseball cap. 'The widow's wardrobe,' he called it. The black wasn't worn as a symbol of grief, but to hide the five pounds he'd gained over the last few weeks. Grief, it seemed, was an insatiable and hungry bitch. Having never been an ounce overweight in his life, he was fascinated by the ridge of fat beneath his abdomen. He thumbed it like the strings of a mandolin. He regarded his new heft — the slight concave arc of his lanky figure — as a physical manifestation of sorrow.

Cheap antiseptic stank up the van. Sal closed his eyes, inhaled, alert to smells other than the disinfectants attempt to mask the traces of sour milk. He sniffed the hairs on the back of his hand, noting Randy's scent in his own perspiration — the honeyed reek that clings to the dying like overripe fruit. Maybe the smell emanated from the sleigh bed where Randy had spent the last months of his life. Sal ran his hand over the curvature of the baseboard. He sniffed his fingertips. The odor there, pervasive, also wafted from his palm, his wrist, his forearm. He stank of sour sweat, flowery soap. His aroma, distasteful and familiar — terminal, he thought — spoke to him of an intimacy he would never allow himself again, except with death.

Randy's been gone so long, Sal thought, *it can't be his scent on my skin.*

"It must be my own."

*   *   *

"He's early," Barbara said, peeking through the curtains.

"Why hasn't he gotten out of the van?" Ben asked.

"Just go see what he's doing."

Neither left the foyer. They paced the marble — Ben in scruffy loafers with rubber soles that squeaked, Barbara in pink silk slippers that brushed the floor beneath a light step. Had Sal seen them through the gray screen door he might have mistaken their movements for a slow lover's waltz.

"This is ridiculous," Ben said.

Barbara smiled, touched her husband's hand. A white short-sleeve dress shirt made him seem scrawnier than he was. He had the wiry, slack arms of an old man.

Ben considered his wife curiously. "I'm nervous about seeing him," he said. "Everything reminds me of Randy."

"It could be worse," she said.

"How so?"

Since the funeral, Barbara had not been able to tell her husband that she was having trouble with the simplest memories of their son.

"It just could," she said.

This had been the longest conversation they'd had since the funeral. She pressed a finger against his mouth. His sweet breath was tempered by a whiff of something metallic — hot steel, aluminum, an alloy in the process of rusting. He smelled like fear, like sadness. Mourning, like a tenacious flu, had entered his body weeks ago and was leaving him, slowly, as he exhaled. She kept her own sorrow balled tight in the pit of her stomach, sadness festering in acids. *My own breath must be rancid*, she thought. She cupped her hand over her mouth and exhaled.

"Don't worry," Ben told her. "Your breath's as fresh as daisies."

Barbara thought how naturally, how openly Ben had wept at Randy's funeral, of her own public stoicism at the graveside. How she had wanted to scream and how that would just not do! So she'd set her jaw, met the eye of all who glanced her way. Even behind her black veil, the one she purchased in Cedar Rapids because all the Waterloo fabrics were polyester blends, she knew they could see her stare: steely in the face of death. Hadn't she wanted the neighbors to find her noble, tragic even? People were, fundamentally, ugly. She herself could be cruel. Randy's death, its *distasteful* source, would be a reflection on *her*. Small town folk had nothing better to do than gossip about the dead fag. In her own humble way, Barbara felt she had diverted attention away from Randy. His death wasn't about the shame of AIDS, but resilience: the indomitable spirit of the living. That's what people would talk about. She'd made certain of it.

In the hallway, she smiled.

"How can you look so happy?" Ben asked.

Barbara tensed. "It must be a trick of the light."

"That's your natural glow," Sal said, tapping faintly at the door. The loose screen rattled. *Keep it light*, he thought. *And brief.*

Ben could feel small talk coming on. The cheery timbre of his voice startled him. "I've been meaning to fix that," he said about the door.

"When you're done there," Sal said, patting Ben on the shoulder, "maybe you can fix the van."

"What's wrong with it?" Ben asked.

"You name it."

"You want some coffee?" Barbara offered.

"No, thanks." He wanted to get as far as possible before sundown. If he left Waterloo before noon, he'd be halfway through Nebraska by nightfall. He'd brought tapes to keep him awake, all new music that had no associations with Randy.

Though Ben had only seen Sal once before today — at the quilt — he'd noticed the subtle, nearly imperceptible changes to his countenance.

"You okay?" Ben asked, watching Sal shift from foot to foot. "You seem distracted."

Sal braced himself. He didn't want to seem impatient. He put his feet flatly on the floor, the way he always did before lying, as if the feel of solid earth beneath him would ground his deceit. "I'd like to make it back to Chicago before dark. I hate driving at night."

"Right, then," Ben said, and headed out the door and towards the van.

.   .   .

Barbara followed them no further than the door. How much help could a petite woman in pink slippers be? She watched Sal walk towards the van, upright and purposeful. Behind him strode the skinny form of her husband, a touch of scoliosis in his posture. Thirty years difference between the two men couldn't mask their striking physical similarities. They looked to her like timed exposures of a single object. Same height, same build, same determined gait. Ben could be Sal's much older brother. Why hadn't she recognized this before?

She wondered if her son had noticed.

Sal, at the foot of the porch, caught her eye when he nearly dropped a cardboard box as he lowered it to the ground. He looked at her, his eyebrows arched. His face was part apology, part provocation, part...oh, she couldn't tell. "I have no idea what I'm doing," he said to her, his overeager grin impossible to read. There was derision and malice in it, and complicity, too. "It feels kind of good to wing it, doesn't it, Barbara?"

His ambiguity infuriated her. So proper, so civil, and — it was there in his forced cheer and strained camaraderie — so terrified. What kept him so reined in and on edge? Was it the prospect of living alone, adjusting to life without her son? If that were the case, they shared the same misery. Randy's death — the constant, consuming awareness of it — bore down on her. It had been easy, for all these years, to place blame wholly on Sal. He'd become her rationale; the reason she avoided, the reason she retreated, the reason she remained in Iowa when her son was only a few hours away. But now she lived with the waking nightmare that not only close friends, who may already suspect, but those disreputable gossips that had a way of changing a community's perception might discover that she had done nothing, absolutely nothing, to comfort her son.

Nevermind that, she told herself. There was nothing she could do for him now, except honor his memory. This should have been an easy thing to do. But her memory of him consisted of nothing more than fleeting images that came swiftly and confused her. Randy, asleep in his basinet, dressed in full tuxedo. Randy, eight years old, smoking a cigar while trapped beneath a sheet of ice. Randy, acne-scarred at puberty, falling from a skyscraper while filing his nails. There were more, so many of them, none of which made any sense, all of which shared a striking anomaly. No matter what age her son should be in the image — infant, toddler, teenager — he always appeared with the gaunt, haunted face she had seen when they visited Chicago. If she had been with him during his last few months, helped nurse him through the final hours, she might have fresh and painful memories, might be able to remember him as he was, fully, instead of in fragmentary hallucinations.

She saw Sal carrying boxes from the bottomless van, occasionally glancing up to see if she was still watching from the doorway. The grin plastered across his face now struck her, unmistakably, as elation. He looked like a happy man, a man whose conscience was clear. And why not? He did what she couldn't do. He was there, to the end, for her son.

She withdrew from the screen door, its mesh of light and dust. She considered herself a resilient woman, yet she could not have withstood her son's suffering. Sal, though: she could bear his. They could help each other.

She could know him, in a sense, as Randy had, and in that knowing she might still discover the Son she had denied.

* * *

As they unloaded the van, Sal surveyed the mounting objects on the Manning's front yard. It was a pathetic gathering, especially the faded, threadbare cabriolet chairs. Most of these items wouldn't merit a second glance at a garage sale.

Ben tried to help as much as possible, but he felt old and weak, easily winded. He reached for larger pieces anyway, as if intent might translate to strength. When failing to lift the sleigh bed's solid headboard, Sal handed him a more manageable object. "Take this footstool," he told Ben. "I can manage the headboard myself."

Had Sal been watching him struggle? He said little, though his silence wasn't unfriendly. It was vigilant. Were these qualities — similar to those of his wife — what drew his son to Sal? His son's own feelings were as easy to read as flashcards. Ben wondered if Sal's opaque manner challenge Randy, turned him on? He felt a blush cross his cheeks. "I used to be stronger," he said, faltering. He held the footstool against his chest, embracing it. "I was going to convince you of my manliness! Truth be told, I was always something of a weakling, a bit of a — what's the word today?"

"Sissy?" Sal said.

"Wimp," he offered. "Such a wimp! I never knew what I wanted, or felt, or—" He ran his fingernail along a gash in the footstool. "That's not true. I knew how I felt," he grimaced at the tense of the word, "how I *feel* about one thing."

Ben thought he saw a winsome curl on Sal's thin red lips, a subtle confession that they shared the same emotion.

"What's going inside first?" Sal asked, pointing to the bounty on the lawn. He jumped out of the van, wiping his dusty hands across his black shirt, leaving a smudge of fingerprints.

Ben checked the items on the lawn. Except for the handmade red toy chest, everything was ugly — their only value lay in having once belonged to his son. Glancing into the empty van, he noticed a small overnight suitcase beneath the passenger seat. Was Sal planning to spend the night? Ben recalled him saying he wanted to return to Chicago before dusk. Maybe the suitcase held more of Randy's things — clothes, or tax receipts — and it had gotten lodged under the seat during the drive.

"What about that?" Ben pointed.

"That's mine," Sal said, too quickly, his tone sharp. He felt the muscles strain in his face. There was an ache in his cheekbones, behind his ears. He smiled to soften his manner, but only seemed more anxious. "Let's just get this stuff in the house so I can get back to Chicago."

Ben knew he was lying. It was in his posture, in each deliberate movement counter to his natural grace. How much strength it took Sal to deceive! Why was that? Ben wanted more time with him so he might know. He wanted to learn to read the contradictions of his character — his petty dislikes, irrational joys, whatever emotional shadings lit him up or doused his ardor. Ben found Sal both subtle and vulgar. He didn't want to be robbed of the opportunity to discover why that was. He wanted to piece Sal together in much the same way Randy had, and to uncover aspects of his son in the process.

He grabbed a chair by its leg. He stomped towards the stand-alone garage where he would store all but one of Randy's belongings. They would gather dust there, rot from humidity. Years from now, already abandoned, they would be forgotten.

*   *   *

The door to Ben's study was stuck, swollen with humidity. Sal, carrying one end of the red toy chest, turned his side to the door and popped it open with a thrust of his hip.

"Oooh," he said. "I wasn't the Halsted Street Disco Queen of '77 for nothing!"

He backed into the study, Ben following. The room was dank. Even when Ben switched on the swag lamp above the desk, the space was still dark, enclosed by rough wood paneling. There was a hum in the room; a humidifier maybe, not visible to Sal. Was this the place that Ben retreated when he'd call Sal to check on Randy's health?

"Where do you want this to go?" he asked Ben, the red box heavy between them. Was there a suitable place for a garish red toy chest in a man's study? The furniture around them was weighty and functional, academic except for a fainting coach with plush brocade cushions caked over with dust. This was a room demanding the drift of pipe smoke, a mix of hazelwood and almond tobacco, not the chemically-treated strawberry waft of air freshener that permeated the room and made Sal's nose twitch. Here was a room, Sal thought, to contemplate futures.

"Put it back here for now," Ben decided.

They maneuvered around the desk, Ben losing his grip on the chest. Sal caught Ben's side as it fell, and gently lowered the entire thing onto the floor. He bent down to adjust one of the chest clasps that'd come loose in the tumble. When he straightened back up, he was staring down at Ben's desktop.

Multiple images of a smiling Randy were trapped beneath a Plexiglas covering. Here was a history of Randy's dental care from childhood through college: toothless to gap-toothed, glistening braces to gleaming crowns. Sal recalled Randy smiling right before he died. Sal added to the collage a mental picture of Randy in the last seconds of his life, the gap between his front teeth having returned thanks to the decay of his gums. If he'd only had that photo to complete Ben's collection.

"What a charmer," Ben said, pointing to Randy's first grade photo. "Look at those freckles. That cowlick! He tried to slick it back with spit, but it would — *whoosh* — pop up again with a vengeance." Ben ran a finger over the photo, leaving a mark in the small accumulation of dust. "I don't know why I love this picture." Ben tapped the Plexiglas twice. "Randy *hated* it."

Sal could see why the photo was precious to Ben. For all Randy's physical imperfections here — the boxy haircut that made his head look colossal, the dense tier of freckles across ruddy cheeks — the photo captured his enthusiasm like none Sal had ever seen. Randy's bright eyes were focused past the camera, the photographer, beyond this sterile moment to await the captured surprise of the next picture. There, in his goofy smile, is the expectation of experience, and the promise that — sweeter still — he might share it with you. *How thrilling,* Sal thought, *to have a Son like that! How awful that his hair, spit-backed or mussed, was always defeated by such tragic cowlicks!*

Sal ran his fingertips over Randy's encased image. His hand came to rest near Ben's. Warmth generated between them. Ben's skin had the faint whiff of baby powder. Sal fought back the impulse to hold his hand.

They smiled down at Randy, their two faces mirrored on the scratched surface of the Plexiglas, each of them studying the other's likeness: sad, pensive and, in that delicate reflection, yes, ghostly. Sal moved away from the desk, his likeness vanishing from the plastic casing. For a moment, he saw Randy's radiant six-year-old grin next to Ben's conflicted appearance, proud and grief-stricken, and he felt that they would both be trapped beneath that cold, clear protector forever.

. . .

Fists balled deep in his pockets, Sal waited for Barbara in the street, tapping the curb with the metal tips of his stiff new boots. *Why leave,* he thought sarcastically, *when it's such a lovely afternoon to visit the cemetery?*

He could see Ben and Barbara through the screen door, their lips moving. Were they arguing? Talking about him? Discussing the lone suitcase left in the van? All he could hear was a mumbling, the rumor of words.

"Stay here, Benjamin," Barbara said. "I need time alone with Sal."

"I don't understand."

"Neither do I. Just let me ask him to return to us when he gets sick. We're his—" she stumbled over the word, "-family now. But I need to do this myself."

"You need?"

Sal heard derisive laughter as Ben withdrew from the foyer. He saw Barbara, alone, resting her shoulder against the archway. He stared at her silhouette, elongated. Brutal light ravaged her face. No one had ever looked as lonely to him, as defeated, as she did in that moment.

Yet as soon as she stepped outside, his compassion vanished. She had changed into a yellow sweat suit made preposterous by the addition of glittery gray-silver squiggles. He tried, unsuccessfully, to suppress a vicious laugh.

She stomped past him, tapping his shoulder twice to demand that he follow. She trod the street dead center, no cars or people in sight, her steps deliberate, paced for a jaunt.

Sal scanned the driveway for Ben. The front door was shut. "Isn't Ben coming?" he asked.

Barbara, halfway down the block, didn't answer him or hadn't heard him. He wasn't sure. Hustling to catch up with her, he reached for her arm to slow her down. Before he could ask if Ben would be joining them at the cemetery, two boys appeared from around the corner racing silver mountain bikes.

Barbara felt Sal's hand on her arm. She attempted to pull away, but he tightened his grasp. Firm, gentle. She let herself be slowed.

"Move, Grandma!" one kid yelled, swerving past her. The other flipped her his middle finger and whooped with a girlish squeal. She wanted to smack the little brat, teach him some manners, but the sound — taunting and familiar — reminded her of Randy.

She struggled to catch her breath. "Be careful!" she yelled after them, waving at the boys on their bikes. "Those things are much bigger than when you and Randy were kids."

"They're mountain bikes," he clarified.

Barbara grunted. "Do you see any mountains around here?"

"Of course not, Barbara. No mountains. No Ben."

She snorted, brushing lint from her sleeve.

"Is he okay?" Sal asked.

"He's fine." She waved Sal off.

He crossed his arms against his chest, cradling each elbow in his splayed fingers, forearms pushing down on his stomach.

Barbara noticed the flab gathered at his waist. "Ben's tired," she said, "and I thought you could use the exercise."

Sal sucked in his gut with a slow intake of breath. He bit his upper lip to stop himself from telling her to fuck off.

She knew she'd angered him — what an easy target. "I thought it might be nice to have some time alone together," she said. "To talk."

"Nice," he said, his response curt. He softened his voice, but kept a hint of threat in his muted tone. "Talk then."

"Oh, Sal."

He waited for her to carry on, but she didn't. They walked the rest of the way to the cemetery in silence.

They entered the graveyard, stealing past lines of trees and headstones. The names on the stones struck Sal as ancestral — the Virdens, the Dunsmores, a family of Bluedorns — and unmistakably white. He couldn't imagine Randy, with his flaming hair and outsized personality, ever having felt at home here. Hadn't he once told Sal he thought the state motto should be: 'Iowa — we put the white on rice'?

Barbara pointed out a hillside bluff. The family plot was there, she told him, but she paused at the foot of the rise.

"I was wondering," she said, and reached to take hold of his arm. Though she had rehearsed what she was going to say during the walk here, she didn't still quite know how to start. It had never been easy for Barbara to seek anyone's help. Now she would make up for years of self-reliance by asking Sal for a monster of a favor. What tack could she take — what was the most sincere way — to ask him to return to Waterloo to die? "I was wondering," she repeated. If she simply asked him, would he give her the opportunity to do what she could for him? Or might he deny her, aware that this would be her only chance to reconcile what little she'd done for her son?

"Before he died, Randy asked me if I — if we, Ben and I — would take care of you when you got ill."

She heard the escalation in her voice, the falseness of it, and watched as Sal's long face turned harsh, sour.

Whatever chance she'd had with him was gone, evaporating with the echo of her lie.

He was horrified — not by the offer, which touched him enough to consider it for a second — but by the ruthlessness of the bait.

"That's *kind* of you," he said, with a strained formality that could not veil his anger. She should have just told him that she needed him. It wouldn't have swayed his decision, but he could have left with a respect for her courage, her sorrow, her honesty.

Barbara neared her son's grave with its plain and understated headstone. There was something spray-painted there, some dismal graffiti, but as she got closer to read it, she froze in her tracks.

AIDS KILLS FAGS DEAD.

Sal ran into her, nearly knocking her off her feet. "Are you okay?" he asked, grabbing her arms to keep her from falling.

She didn't answer.

Sal scanned the family plot, reading the names there — Sophie, Johnson, an Ebenezer for Christ's sake! — before he got to Randy's. He didn't notice the graffiti at first, just the headstone, polished to a fault, with surface etchings that were simple, fresh.

Randall Patrick Manning
1952-89
Loving Son & Companion

There was a flutter of crows, and the low chug of a crop-duster circling nearby, and other common distractions — cars in the distance, tractors roiling through upturned soil, yet his eye kept returning to the words in stone, their stark fucking finality, and his place, implied, among them. *Loving Son. Companion.* Simple, harmless words.

But the ampersand! *&*!

It angered and touched him equally; the presumption of it, right, and also the warmth of it. The act of inclusion was the meaning of its very design — the way the symbol doubled back upon itself in embrace. Sal recognized this as Ben's doing, down to the stress of the italics, but Barbara, tight-lipped, must surely have consented.

When he finally saw the defacement, the first thing he noticed was its artlessness. Lines of spray from a canister blended into words, a paraphrase of a marketing slogan for a pesticide: **AIDS Kills Fags Dead**. He — it had to have been a teenage boy, wasn't it always? — had drawn a red aerosol canister with thick streaks of black spray fanning out from the silver nozzle. Beneath the lethal mist lay stickmen on their backs, spindly legs extended like dying insects, the anger and sexual panic in the picture obvious, sophomoric, misdirected.

As he got closer, he could smell fumes on the headstone. The paint was fresh, most likely done this morning. The sketching — with its direct lines and ugly implications, its in-your-face spirit — brought Randy to him more fully than any photograph or memory. He could hear Randy cackling at its idiotic symbolism, and could imagine that, later on, safe at home, they might have wondered why someone with true potential would waste such talent on hateful drivel.

Sal reached towards the headstone to touch the letter 'A'.

"No." Barbara shoved his hand away.

"Why?"

Barbara had no answer. She wanted to stare at the offensive thing, scan it for clues. Who would dare be so insensitive to her, so vicious to her son? Could it have been those little bastards on their mountain bikes? Their tires were muddy and wet. They acted as if they were racing away from something.

"Those fucking kids!" she yelled.

"What kids?" Sal at first thought she was referring to the teenagers responsible for the graffiti until he remembered the boys on their bicycles. He found Barbara's indignation, righteous at it was, belated and grossly insufficient. Where was her fortitude when her son was struggling to breathe? "Those kids couldn't have been more than 8 years old. They don't think about girls, let alone homos."

"What kind of person does this?" she asked.

Sal ran his thumb along the red letter 'A'. The paint was warm from the sun. Still wet, the paint smudged his thumb.

"Don't," Barbara pleaded. She wanted to call the police, have them dust for fingerprints, round up everyone in town, take statements. "You're tampering with evidence."

"Evidence of what?"

"Of what?" she asked, incredulous. "Of hatred? Of intolerance?"

"You forgot 'hypocrisy'," Sal snapped, no longer trying to mask his irritation.

Barbara took a step back, stunned. Who the hell was he to talk to her this way? She marched towards him and stood in his shadow — the hearty old woman flanked by the towering gargoyle.

"We have to find out who did this," she insisted.

"It doesn't matter."

"Of course it matters, you dirty faggot."

Sal laughed. "You think that hurts?"

Barbara slapped his face with such force that her own hand grew numb.

He didn't move, though the blow caused the flesh to ripple across his check. "Is that the best you can do?" He grabbed Barbara's hand, the one she had just used to hit him. He lifted her hand towards his face to smack him again, but she pulled her arm away. There was a red mark on her palm from the paint on his thumb.

"Go ahead. Hit me. Call me names. You think calling me a 'faggot' insults me? Well here's an irony to get your head around, Barbara: that kind of ugliness may be the only thing left that I'm immune to."

Sal was wrong — Barbara knew it. She could see that the flush upon his cheek was not caused solely by her hand. Her words, her invective, inflamed him. *Hate, ignorance,* she thought, *it began so early, left too late.*

She turned away.

Sal took hold of her, brought her close to him. He lifted his hand towards her face, guiding her chin up to look in his eyes. "AIDS KILLS FAGS DEAD. It was your son's dirty secret. You think it's yours now. But it's always been yours, Barbara. Randy didn't have secrets, just amusements. Your son — my lover — he would have laughed, laughed the way he did at everything painful."

There was a cloudiness in her eyes, a rheumy shield he had never noticed before. It was nature, he thought, protecting the elderly from seeing any more suffering by hazing their view. He himself would die young, alone. Clear-eyed.

"Oh, Barbara," he whispered, releasing her. "If you only knew."

"I know my son—"

"You know nothing."

She opened her mouth to protest. All she could manage was a bleat of words, an incoherent choke. She was weeping — from grief, from shame. She couldn't tell. It didn't matter. There were tears, and they flowed!

She let Sal gather her into his arms, against his chest. She felt only his embrace, and the brutal palpitations of her rigid body while she cried in his arms, bewilderingly, just like her son must have once cried and felt reassured, not abandoned, never judged.

Part Two

In-Between Days

Patchwork
Part Two

DUSK HAD COME by the time Sal pulled away from the Manning's Washington Avenue curb and down the perfectly innocuous suburban street. In his rearview mirror he saw them waving, illuminated beneath a streetlamp that appeared more like their own personal spotlight. He wouldn't be surprised if he'd found out that Barbara had called the electric company for the sole purpose of having the light come on early, changed out for a higher wattage, and adjusted for maximum impact in order to ensure that the image of them unknowingly waving their final goodbyes — she and Ben — would be implanted in his mind forever. Barbara was crafty that way. And though Sal had stuck his arm out the window as he turned toward the exit for the 218, his hand cupped and moving side-to-side as if he were a Papal envoy offering them his impersonal benediction, he was shocked to find that, when he looked into the rearview before changing lanes, the solitary image of the two of them — waving away and bathed in light — was still there.

He drove southwest in a near zigzag pattern. He had no maps, no fixed destination in mind, just the impetus to get away, get ahead, put some distance between his past and a loneliness, both intangible and concrete, that had not begun to manifest yet was still — stunning as daybreak and absolute as nightfall — always encroaching. It was near 3:00 a.m. when he saw the skyline of Kansas City ahead of him and almost an hour later when its downtown lights faded behind him, swiftly being waved on by the vision of Barbara and Ben in his rearview mirror. He blinked to banish their image away, rubbed the tiredness from his eyes, but there they were, his lover's parents vacantly bidding him goodbye, as tenacious as sunspots.

He drove until he had just passed through Topeka, Kansas, stopping at some dilapidated rest-stop whose bathrooms stank of fermented urine and whose only choice of nutrition came in a vending machine near empty save for a packet of Fig Newton's and a fully stocked row of corn nuts. The sun was just rising, but the day, already fetid with humidity, was suffocating. He rolled down the windows of the van as he got back on I-70.

He didn't stop until he reached Denver, Colorado that afternoon: no humidity, not a cloud in the sky and, fuck, no oxygen! It took him a moment to acclimate to the Mile High City's thin atmosphere before heading out to find a cheap motel. He wasn't on a budget — he'd pocketed a significant sum for the sale of his business and was also surprised to find, not to mention touched, that he'd been the sole beneficiary of Randy's life insurance policy. Still, he only required the services of a hot shower and a modest bed to take a few hours nap. From what he'd seen of Denver in the entire half an hour he'd been there, he wouldn't be staying. It was too clean, too hard to breathe, too white. Sure, the mountains were pretty, but he didn't require beauty in a city — he needed edge, funkiness, diversity, and at least one superior Chinese restaurant that delivered. There might have been a place with savory Mu Shu Pork in Denver in 1990, yet in the six blocks he'd walked in the lower downtown area — or LoDo, as it came to be known — he didn't see a storefront or menu featuring the impenetrable calligraphy of Sinitic characters. He returned to his room, napped, showered, and headed back onto I-70, Barbara and Ben signaling him on to the freeway from their vaporous perch inside the rearview frame.

And he drove, this time northwest to Salt Lake City, in a sorry attempt to outwit a past that was not only in his head and his heart but in his blood, that viciously viscous matter which would mutate, insinuate and, sometime in the future — ha! *the future!* — destroy him. He couldn't drive fast enough nor long enough to change what had happened, to alter what was coming, to escape a void he'd been denying the last six weeks and that now seemed to be riding shotgun as he barreled down the I-15 into the verdant Salt Lake Valley. No, this city full of Mormons and impeccable vistas and a climate similar to that of Chicago wouldn't do. So he found the nearest exit, u-turned beneath the underpass, and got back on the I-15, driving ten hours straight with stops only for the restroom, a drive-thru burger and a cup, and then another cup, of coffee.

Then there it was, Phoenix, with its uninspired architecture, its mall-ish neighborhoods, and that parched, unyielding heat. And there it went, a desert oasis of prefabricated ugliness, bid adieu by the parents-in-law who either appeared in the mirror like a shimmering vision or were summoned by Sal's own imagination to give credence to his subconscious desire to flee. It was hard for him to tell at this point. But still he moved west towards the mountains of California, five hours this time, rest areas farther apart from each other, the warmth in the van insufferable due to an air-conditioning unit that worked — if worked was the right word — when it felt like it, which was rarely and weakly, forcing Sal to stop at a high-desert convenience mart for a pair of scissors and a block of ice that now sat in the passenger seat along with his void, the nothingness and everything-ness of Randy, and he chipped away at it, the abyss he was feeling, of course, but mostly the ice, holding the cold shavings along the nape of his neck, the water melting down his shoulders, dripping into the cotton t-shirt that was soon sopped and clammy, only to dry just as quickly as he made his descent towards the arid valley and whirligig energy turbines, monstrous clusters of technological sentinels that ushered him toward the vast faked green vision of Palm Springs, where he stayed just long enough for an afternoon breakfast of runny eggs, limp bacon, hash browns and coffee — always coffee — one more cup of coffee, all the while being stared at by elderly variations of Ben and Barbara, their skin stretched tight across the tanned canvas of their faces, and he in days-old jeans and a t-shirt that was both wrinkled and rank.

"Waitress, check please," he said, before hitting the head and, again, the road.

And who knows? He may have gone along like this for another few days, weeks, months even — he really wasn't sure and he honestly didn't mind — but his devil-may-care road trip met with a force far greater than any stimulus, momentum, or irrational actions of a man whose grief had no direction, no antecedent, no almanac,

no atlas, no understanding, no end-in-sight: just the fun-
neling, then the thickening, then the slowing of Los Angeles traffic, thousands of cars in lockstep on a series of
interconnecting highways, freeways, clover-shaped off-
ramps and eight-lane boulevards like a concrete girdle
that kept the sprawling city from being shaken off the
face of the earth.

As he approached Sunset Boulevard — the windows
down, the van full of toxic exhaust, the radio blasting
an alternative nugget from a band called, ironically, he
thought, The Cure — the cars came to a sudden and complete stop. He laughed — from exhaustion, exaspera-
tion, sleep-deprivation, whatever — and knew that if he
looked in his rearview mirror, the Mannings would be
nowhere to be found.

Part Three
1999

"Rose leaves, when the rose is dead,
Are heap'd for the belovèd's bed;
And so thy thoughts, when thou art
    gone,
Love itself shall slumber on."

                    — Percy Bysshe Shelley,
            "Music, When Soft Voices Die"

Patchwork

Part Three; Chapter One

IN 1998, AT the antiseptic Pavilions in the gay heart of Los Angeles, West Hollywood, Sal, now 48-years-old, was shopping last minute for vegetables for that evening's dinner date. He preferred the low-tech ambiance — or, as he'd call it, "sleaze" — of "Rockin'" Ralph's in Hollywood. But he didn't have time to drive east simply for the chance of spotting some underfed, leather-faced hair-metal has-been stashing a liter of Stoli inside a cart full of organics intended to make him — the old rock star — look health-conscious and not like the burnt-out ex-junkie alcoholic he no doubt was.

No time — today at least — for that. Sal's date tonight was his first since coming to Los Angeles. Oh, he'd had plenty of escapades, encounters — words you'd name a gay bar or use to describe sexual conquests. It was easy to get laid in West Hollywood: you could just stroll down Santa Monica Boulevard for a beer and a quick chat, or, by mid-decade, dialup on online chat-room and scroll through a menu of delicacies like you were ordering in a delivery meal — hmm, what to have tonight? Mexican, Italian, French? Sex was everywhere; all you needed was the desire, a box of condoms, and you were set. It seemed to Sal you could hardly get through Pavilions without someone trying to pick you up! (This may be why he preferred Ralph's. Sometimes he really did only want a cucumber.) He was no prude; his number of sexual partners both pre-, during, and post-Randy would certainly fall on the high end of a grading curve, though he'd always found it all compulsory, less so now in his forties, a lot of work for very little payoff, even when the "work" involved was simply waiting for the squeal and flutter of the phone line to give way to an internet connection.

But tonight he had a full-on date, the first time since leaving Chicago eight years ago that he'd invited anyone to his place for an intimate meal. He was an expert cook. Italian dishes his specialty. What else with a last name like Gagliardo? But he hadn't made a formal meal in ages, especially one where the desired effect was to impress — no, seduce — a man. Normally so nonchalant, today he was nervous as a teen, walking the Pavilions aisles with a jittery distraction.

"Can I help you?" A stockboy — so pretty he looked as if he'd stepped out of the pages of International Male, not from the grocery store break room — was staring at Sal, who must have seemed lost. The aisle was overstuffed with gourmet breads from the LaBrea and Boudin bakeries. The earthy smell of yeast saturated the air; the odors of *panettone, ciabatta, strucia, chapitas. Whatever happened to just French and Italian?* Sal wondered. The heady scent of bread was a warning to all gay men that here was an accretion of fat-inducing carbohydrates, and Sal noticed both the flurry of sounds elsewhere in the store and the desolate length of this empty aisle.

"Sir?" the stockboy asked.

Who the hell is 'sir'? Sal thought. *Not me. I'm only 48, you little — what did they call them now? — Twinkie.* He much preferred the 70's designation of 'chicken'.

"Tell me this," Sal said, gazing down at the perfectly coiffed, rosy-cheeked piece of fluff that passed as the ideal of gay masculinity in the 90's. "What exactly is *focaccia* bread?"

The stockboy explained, with great animation, the distinctions between *focaccias* and *ciabattas* — mixing techniques, baking processes.

Sal listened intently, flicking his middle finger off his thumb as if zapping at a pest. *The model employee*, he thought, and smiled benevolently. But when the stockboy began an analysis of semolina versus whole-wheat flour, Sal grew impatient with the boy's officious, superior tone. "How do you know all this?"

"My ex was a baker in San Francisco," he said, not as a matter of fact, but dismissively, almost sorely.

"Oh," Sal said, thinking he noted a wounded tone in the stockboy's voice. Had he lost a lover, too? Had he weathered the first cusp of the AIDS crisis, lucky to live through the 80's and into the 90's with its new cocktail of medications and its renewed hope for life? Though Sal knew full well it was none of his business, he asked the Pavilions employee if his ex, too, had died.

The stockboy paused a moment to consider Sal's question before answering. "No," he said, adding smugly, "He got fat." He said this as if that were the worst possible fate in the world, which, Sal realized — this being Los Angeles — it probably was.

"How tragic," Sal said, before changing the subject. "Where can I find Brussels sprouts?"

Sal halved the vegetables on the prep counter, along with a fresh clove of minced garlic. He was going to brown it all in olive oil, then let the aromatic sprouts heat over a low simmer until perfection.

The kitchen itself was small yet functional; one of the apartment's selling points for him when he'd decided to stay in Los Angeles. He thought he'd end up in San Francisco — he'd been there once, a teenage runaway, and loved its anything-goes vibe, its intellectual free-for-all — but had never been to Southern California. The lure of the City of Angels — to visit at least — was as strong to Sal as the proverbial siren to a sailor. L.A held the promise of warm weather. The excitement of celebrity glamour. Mountains, beaches, valleys. Anything, really, you could ask for in a landscape to keep the eye refreshed, unlike the monotonous lull of the Midwestern horizon. Best of all, L.A. felt expendable to him. Modern and functional. Built for the moment only. A one-night stand he could leave without the slightest tinge of regret.

Once he had found himself before dusk on Mulholland Drive. Fire blazed in the distance. The Biblical flames atop the San Gabriel crest to the east were serpentine, spellbinding. Raging smoke mixed with the constant San Fernando smog as he stood there — open-mouthed — marveling at a sunset gloried by devastation.

But the telling detail of the city, for him at least, was not the spectacle of ruin displayed for his entertainment, but the domestic scenes in the houses and patios leading to the Valley below: kids swimming in oversized pools; husbands barbecuing; friends sipping pre-meal martinis while toasting to those poor unfortunates to the east while still enjoying the view.

This, he had thought, *would be an ideal place to die.*

So he found an apartment – a small one bedroom on the cusp of West Hollywood – and waited. He'd brought nothing with him from Chicago except the textile prints he'd saved from college. He didn't see the need to surround himself with sentimental objects when he'd had no idea how long he might live. Randy had gone quickly – two years from diagnosis to death – and Sal believed he'd deteriorate along much the same timeline. He purchased what was necessary, only when it was needed. A breakfast table and chairs (a mess when he got them, but now fashionably distressed). A futon he used for a few months as a bed until he could stand it no longer and bought a basic box spring and mattress. Dishes. Glasses. Utilitarian items. He lived prudently – investing the money from Randy's insurance policy, which he'd tripled in three years time. He had his own savings from the sale of his business. And there was the monthly consulting fee he received from Billy Bud's in Chicago simply to fax them sketches of original, seasonal arrangements.

He went to the beach. The preening circus of Venice was his favorite. He loved the strange juxtaposition of exhibitionists lifting weights at the outdoor gym while anorexic meth addicts begged for change on the same oceanfront block. He himself had taken up hiking, slimming down from the weight he'd put on in Chicago. He went to the movies since he didn't own a television.

And after all those days in the sun and all those walks and all those shitty, shitty films — *Dances with Wolves won the goddamned Oscar®!* — he was in the best physical health of his life, though mildly dejected about the state of American cinema. The Best Picture win for *The Silence of the Lambs*, much more to his liking, was a boon, as was the introduction of antiretroviral drugs — protease inhibitors, specifically. He was not just living well, but thriving.

So he went shopping for more permanent furniture. His tastes had simplified since Chicago. Everything he bought was comfortable, minimal, in neutral tones. He hadn't grown mystical or even recognizably spiritual, though he found himself drawn to eastern design. The living area pieces were all close to the ground. The breakfast nook was demolished, replaced with Japanese Edo tables and floor cushions, which took no small amount of commitment from him as he was a tall man.

*   *   *

He checked on the balsamic vinaigrette mushroom chicken simmering in the oven, and was placing the Brussels sprouts in the olive oil and garlic when he heard a faint tap at his front door. 7:30, on the dot. He wasn't sure why he was surprised, but he was. Eduardo was both gay and Asian; Sal expected him to split the difference between the eastern love of punctuality with the gay credo of being fashionably, not to mention rudely, late. By his calculation, he thought he'd have another twenty-two and a half minutes of prep time.

But when Sal opened the door, there was Eduardo, dressed casually yet crisply in pressed jeans and a soft lavender button-down shirt that was tight across his muscular chest. He was a head smaller than Sal; short by anyone's standards, but thick as a wrestler. His round head was closely cropped in the popular Caesar cut of the day, balanced by the shadow of a goatee at his chin. His shirtsleeves were rolled up. He cradled a single gladiola in his arms. The flower — its petals a shade darker than his purple shirt — rested gently against an overdeveloped forearm.

And this is how he handed the gift to Sal, as if passing him a delicate infant.

"Eduardo," Sal said, touched by the single flower.

"Yes?"

He was so serious, so formal. Not as blithe and kind as at the coffee bar where he worked, where Sal had met him and spent months engaged in ambiguous, flirtatious conversation. Though Sal thought Eduardo might be attracted to him, he — Eduardo — had not made one overture to suggest they continue their brief, fraught talks beyond the coffee shop. Sal, buzzing with caffeine from too many lattes one morning, had asked him over for dinner. And here he was.

"Yes?" Eduardo repeated.

"Nothing." Sal leaned in to admire the gladiola, its deep lavender skin, its suggestively half-open/half-closed petals. "Come in."

He led Eduardo into the living room. Its drab simplicity seemed suddenly plain and uninviting to Sal. The only splash of color was this man, and the flower he

111

had brought. "Let me get a vase for this, but, please, sit down."

While searching for a container — he didn't have one vase anywhere — he watched Eduardo round the living room as if there were items of interest in it. Sal imagined it must have been a disappointment to him, this blank space with nothing of personality to read into it, no *objet d'art* for inference, conjecture. Maybe he was thinking that Sal was a very mysterious man. Or an ascetic. Or just cheap. But when he poked his head into the kitchen, he didn't ask about the Spartan arrangements in the apartment.

"Smells delicious," Eduardo said. "What are you cooking?"

"You're not a vegetarian, are you?" Sal asked, alarmed.

He shook his head 'no'. "What is it?"

"Eduardo," he said, gently, "you know a cook relies on the element of surprise."

"Tell me," Eduardo said, his compact body stoical. "Don't be coy."

Sal's shoulders inched up, catlike, ready to pounce — he was a fierce protector in his kitchen — but he relaxed when Eduardo unleashed a silly and feminine giggle, a sound incongruous with his tough look. *Well,* Sal thought, *he is wearing a lavender shirt.* "Sit down. We'll be eating in a few minutes."

"No," he said, head cocked. "You can tell a lot about a person by the way they work. Carry on."

Sal arranged the food and placed the supper plates across from each other, but when he took his place, Eduardo slid his plate next to Sal's and knelt on the floor beside him. It was a bold, intimate move; exciting and unsettling to Sal since he wanted to be able to look at Eduardo, gauge his reactions in conversation, while they dined.

Not that they talked a lot. It wasn't silence, exactly, just unforced companionship. It felt odd to Sal at first — his experience was that people talked as much to let you know they were interesting as when they actually had something to say. Yet Eduardo seemed unconcerned with that. He was content to eat the chicken over its bed of rice pilaf, the braised potatoes with rosemary, and, tentatively, the Brussels sprouts. "What are these?" he asked.

"You're kidding, right?"

"No."

"How old are you? How can you have never seen Brussels sprouts?"

"I'm 27. And I was raised in a cave in the provinces of Cebu." He giggled again, obviously enjoying his ruse. "How old are you?"

"Old enough, young man."

"To be my father."

Sal hit him on the knee.

"Hey!" Eduardo jumped back, then immediately took his place again at the table. "You must be very old not to answer. Or have you forgotten the question already, Grandfather?"

In the living room after the meal, there was more silence, Eduardo content to lean back on the sofa with Sal cross-legged on the floor near his feet. Sal found that that Eduardo was not shy, exactly, but needed the prompting of questions, the bold query of a listener's expectations. He wanted to ask him why he had come tonight, why he'd accepted his invitation as willingly as if he'd just ordered another coffee, but all that came out of his mouth was, "Why?"

And Eduardo, sensing Sal's discomfort, knew the context of the question. He told Sal that he'd always been drawn to older men. He didn't have to play foolish circuit games or lose himself in a meth-induced K-hole just for the pleasure of the company of men his own age. "Guys my own age," he said to Sal, "they are just stupid."

"Yourself excepted, of course," Sal said.

"How do you mean?" Eduardo asked, but he didn't wait for clarification.

His own father was American, his mother from the Philippines. He was distant; she, smothering. Eduardo's attraction to more mature guys was probably a result of Daddy's coldness, but it might also be because they knew what they were doing in bed. He grew up in Minnesota, and was very much an American, though Americans treated him as an outsider and full-blood Asians considered him a "Twinkie."

"You're too old to be a Twinkie," Sal said.

"A gay Twinkie, yes. But in Asian culture a 'Twinkie' is someone who is yellow on the outside, white on the inside."

He told Sal about his disastrous coming out to his mother. She threw lumpia egg rolls across the kitchen at him, collapsing in the middle of the floor to wail. She made him promise never to tell his father. He talked about his bad luck with men, his studies of acupuncture and massage therapy, his best friend from childhood who also moved to Los Angeles and now lived with him.

Sal watched him as he spoke — how matter of fact and gentle his tone, how simple his gestures to punctuate a point. He told Sal all of those getting-to-know-you items of interest Sal thought they might have discussed during dinner. Minus the giggle, there was nothing overtly "gay" about him. The lavender shirt would be disastrous on a more feminine man, but on Eduardo it accentuated his depth of skin tone. His round face was plain — dark oval eyes, upturned nose, small mouth — but malleable when he was animated, and — whether active or in repose — fascinating to ponder. It occurred to Sal — as Eduardo finished the story of his mother's hysterical response to his homosexuality, a story he told by gesturing once as if flinging eggrolls — that Eduardo was as simple and uncomplicated as this room.

Though not without guile or expectation. He must have misread Sal's lengthy silence, because he moved in to kiss him, his lips soft, barely perceptible, enticingly gentle. Yet when he opened his mouth to move in with his tongue, Sal placed a hand on his chest and pushed him, tenderly, back. He had not told Eduardo that he was HIV-positive. He didn't think this was the right time for that conversation.

"Do you want to go out?" Eduardo asked, nonplussed.

Sal wasn't up for a bar. He hesitated.

"Trust me," Eduardo said. "I will surprise you, Sal Gagliardo, Master Chef, bringer of Brussels sprouts."

They stood on the observation deck of the Griffith Park Observatory, the night clear and — Sal noticed — star-studded. The staccato downtown skyline was punctuated by klieg lights. The boxy outline of the Century City grid to the west snaked with traffic.

"If you look very hard," Eduardo said, "I think you can see the ocean tonight."

Sal couldn't see anything but city lights and traffic jams, the helicopters circling in the night sky, though he admired the romantic notion that the Pacific was visible.

"Sometimes," Eduardo said, "I come here to look down at all the little people."

"I can look down at the little people whenever I want."

"That's because you are very tall and I am just a teensy Filipino. I could probably blow you standing up."

Sal had no idea if this was a proposition — he didn't yet know how to fully read Eduardo — but the salaciousness nagged at him. "Is that why we're here?"

"I don't need to drive to Griffith Park to give a blow job. I mean, I could — it is Griffith Park, after all — but that's not why we're here." He took Sal's hand, placed it in his. Together, he swept their arms from east to west. "When I first came to L.A., I wondered, what's the attraction? For me, of course. But also for all these other people we're here to look down upon."

"You're an odd bird, Eduardo."

"No." He moved closer to Sal, resting his hand in the small of Sal's back. "I'm average. I have modest ambitions." He stared west, all the way to the beach, the sand, the lapping, voracious water. "But I didn't know that when I came here. I see that ocean and I think this is where people bring their dreams to die." He put his arm around Sal's waist, squeezed him, and hooked his fingertips into the top of Sal's front right pocket, something no one had done since Randy.

"What dream have you come to bury, Sal?"

Patchwork
Part Three; Chapter Two

THEY DIDN'T HAVE sex — not oral, not penetrative — for three months, and it wasn't because Sal or Eduardo didn't have the desire. There were lots of clinches — hugging, kissing, wrestling, rubbing. And an equal number of what Sal thought of as "close calls." There were kisses that trailed from lips to neck to nipples to the soft and furry pleasure trail below the navel. There was dry humping that escalated in ecstatic velocity. They'd often stop, catch their breath, and reconsider a parameter that neither had discussed though both accepted without much questioning.

Sal wanted to take it to the next level, but never fully decided how to disclose his H.I.V. status. He hadn't given it much thought. Or, more accurately, he'd never had to think about it, account for it to another person.

Eduardo had to be considered.

And here is where Sal froze. Certainly he felt tenderly towards Eduardo. He'd no sooner put him at risk for the virus than he would allow himself to be rejected as a less than desirable boyfriend. That he cared at all was a touching, welcome surprise. But his hesitancy bothered him. He felt both cowardly and prudent. Before he disclosed anything, he wanted Eduardo to be engaged to the point where he couldn't just walk away, unless

Eduardo was a heartless bastard, which Sal could hardly imagine. It didn't seem to be the case when they were making out, Eduardo tugging at Sal's belt, fondling the packed erection beneath the fabric of his jeans. When Sal would gently move himself away, break the clinch for a moment's perspective, Eduardo — with a characteristic patience that Sal thought of as almost courtly — would reach over to run his smooth palm across Sal's warm cheek and say, with a resignation that sounded almost hopeful, "I understand."

But Sal didn't see how he could. He imagined that if he were the frustrated partner, he might scheme, grow petulant, throw a monster tantrum that would shake the rafters. He considered that Eduardo's willingness to wait might be generational — a rift between their ages. Sal was the older man to whom sex was paradoxically predatory and easy; Eduardo the younger man who'd learned about sex in an era where each contact brought the possibility of death to the forefront of consciousness.

So it was with a dirty cackle of relief that Sal found out that Eduardo *did* understand. Eduardo had left a box of condoms on his pillow before he left that morning. He also left two brochures: *Safe Sex Tips*, a graphically illustrated foldout; and *Positive/Negative — H.I.V. Men and Their Sero-Positively-Challenged Partners*.

When Eduardo opened the front door to his apartment, Sal couldn't tell by his odd look of surprise if he was glad to see him or a little bit annoyed.

"What are you doing here?" Eduardo asked.

A simple enough question, though Sal was stumped for an answer. Though they'd been seeing each other frequently, Sal hadn't spent much time at Eduardo's duplex, which was in a borderline neighborhood in North Hollywood. It wasn't fear of the crack alley a few blocks down Lankershim Boulevard that kept him away, or his disdain for Eduardo's hysterically cheerful roommate Celeste, a high-school friend who'd come to L.A. to be a hairstylist and ended up a minor character on a highly rated sitcom. No. What kept Sal from Eduardo's own bed was a smaller though more pervasive problem: Eduardo's Lhasa Apso that was named — in a fit of Filipino hubris — Imelda.

But the box of condoms Eduardo had left that morning had liberated Sal — cheery roommate and evil mutt be damned. He fished in his pocket for one of the handful of Trojans he'd thrown in there before heading into the Valley. He dangled the condom between his thumb and index finger, its shiny gold wrapper reflecting the last rays of the evening sun. "I got your message," he said.

"Oh, that." Eduardo smiled while backing away. "I suppose you'd better come in."

The duplex was simply laid out — the living room, kitchen, and half-bathroom on the lower level; two bedrooms and full-bath upstairs. The living room furniture was a hodgepodge of conflict, items thrown together by "temporary" roommates who'd outlasted the utility of Goodwill retreads yet couldn't quite commit to the idea of a more permanent style.

"Hey, y'all," Celeste drawled from the kitchen, her Southern accent a mystery to Sal since he had been told she was from Michigan. She was baking chocolate chip cookies, but stepped away from the oven to greet Sal. "What's going on? What'cha got there?"

He was still dangling the Trojan.

"He brought us a rubber," Eduardo said. "But I think it's for me."

"Well, hallelujah!" Celeste bounded into the living room, wiping her hands on her apron. She was thin and slight and pretty, also Filipino, which made her drawl even more eccentric. She grabbed Sal by the shoulders. "You boys finally gonna get your freak on or what?"

Sal blushed, which he considered odd as he was embarrassed by what he hadn't yet done, and that what had not occurred between he and Eduardo was also, apparently, cause for concern for Celeste. She was beaming, shaking Sal by the shoulders and saying "Hey, all right," like she was the one who was going to get laid, until Eduardo tugged gently on her apron.

"Maybe we can take Imelda for a walk," he said to Sal, all the while pulling Celeste backwards into the kitchen, admonishing her in his native tongue, which she responded to with a fluent, drawl-less Tagalog.

Imelda yelped from the top of the stairs. While Eduardo was still in the kitchen with Celeste, Sal tried to coax her down. "Come on, girl" he said. "Let's go for a walk." He knew that 'walk' was her second favorite word — right after 'treat' — and she would normally bound the one flight of stairs as if airborne. But the dog hated Sal. She stood on the top step barking at him. He didn't take it personally since Imelda was nasty to everyone except her master, whom she adored. Truly this dog — with her long white fur and black mustache that made her look more like Ferdinand Marcos than her namesake — was the gayest thing about Eduardo, especially when he draped her over his enormous forearm to walk her to the nearby park as if her dainty little paws were too good for the harsh sidewalks of North Hollywood.

"Imelda," Eduardo yelled from the kitchen. "Let's go. *Lumakad*!" She flew down the stairs — a mop with wings — pausing to look up at Sal and, he was certain of it, snarl at him before running to Eduardo, who greeted her with his own odd yelps of "There's my baby. That's my *magaling aso*."

Yes, her master doted over her. Each morning he left Sal's bed early to come to North Hollywood, walk and feed her, then head back to his job in a WeHo coffebar as head barista. He did all this by nine o'clock in the morning. And each night he went back to the Valley to spend time with his beloved before coming to Sal's at ten.

"Why don't you bring her to my apartment when you're here?" Sal had suggested early on, before he had met the creature. "You won't have to get up at 6 a.m., and I could walk her during the day."

"If you can get her to come to you, I will," Eduardo said. "But don't count on it."

"It can't be that hard."

"She's a bitch," Eduardo had replied with no acrimony, just the plain tone of fact. "But she's my bitch. And she's loyal."

The sun had set. June fog had settled over the Valley. And the streetlights surrounding the slight few acres of the North Hollywood Park framed its perimeter in a saturated glow. Eduardo — with Imelda draped over his left forearm — leaned close in to Sal, who walked to his right. There was penance in his posture, Sal thought, deference. *For what?* he wondered. *Having confided in Celeste?* Such a stupid girl to have said anything, yet it was of no consequence. Sal felt the warmth of Eduardo's compact body near his own. For the moment he let the eerie magic of the light and fog hold close to them, until Eduardo put the dog down on the grass, where she growled at Sal until a fetid scent from a nearby tree distracted her.

They followed Imelda deeper into the park, the dog a white blur among shadows. Beneath a grove of trees *(what were they? Sal wondered. Oak? Poplars?)* rested a wooden bench with chipping green paint, ornate rusted iron arms. Old and functional. Inviting. It felt like a perfect place to sit and talk.

Sal pulled Eduardo down on the bench next to him. Imelda yapped her disagreement, but didn't wander far from her master.

"How long have you known?" Sal asked.

"This isn't necessary." Eduardo didn't think he sounded defensive, but Sal pressed on.

"How long have you known, Eduardo?"

"I didn't."

"Then why the condoms?" Sal pulled a folded brochure from his back pocket. "And why this? You could have just asked me."

"You could have just told me."

"But I couldn't."

"Why the fuck not?" Eduardo giggled. "Or, more precisely, why not the fuck?" Eduardo heard the petulance in his tone, the snap of barely controlled anger.

"You know, Sal, it's the '90's. You assume certain facts until you're told differently."

"Well, if that's the case, why didn't you turn down my pillow with the Trojans two months ago?"

"Because it wasn't about the sex."

"It wasn't?"

"No," Eduardo said, calling Imelda to come to him in Tagalog. She felt warm and soft and adoring and alive in his arms. "But it is now."

Sal didn't notice just one thing about Eduardo's bedroom but a barrage of things: the room was immaculate, the bed fully made, throw pillows tossed against the headboard just so; the furniture was part of a set and not some Sally Army mix-and-match; there were no piles of dirty clothes in corners; no dog toys strewn across the floor. But these were details Sal took in as he was tumbling atop Eduardo, who pulled him — forcefully — down onto a king-sized mattress too large for the Filipino yet, it seemed, just waiting for someone of Sal's stature to fill it out.

Remember to breathe, Sal thought. *Slow it up.* But it was hard, haha, with Eduardo tugging Sal's belt off, clutching at the buttons of his 501's, and then the appearance of Imelda on the bed, growling and pawing at Sal's leg.

"Imelda, no," Eduardo said, smacking her on the snout. She retreated to a corner of the mattress. "Sal, yes."

But Sal had stopped moving. He was on his knees, jeans halfway down his thighs, his hard cock pouched towards the left side of his pelvis. He saw the dog to his side — she'd buried her nose in the red briefs that

Eduardo had tried to toss on the floor. She was routing and snorting in them, sniffing and licking. She seemed to really like her master's scent. Sal heard the television downstairs grow louder though he didn't think they were being too rambunctious. He noted these facts, and a few more minor details — the askew hang of Venetian blinds, the vaguely Indian flow of the lush comforter beneath them — but these were secondary distractions, absorbed in a flash and instantly forgotten by the more pressing sensation of the throb of his cock, now freed from his underwear, and the blatant desire of the body displayed — delectably — before him.

"What are you doing?" Eduardo asked. He had his hands above his head, locked behind his neck, while his torso writhed upon the dark red fabric.

"I'm looking at you," Sal said, gazing down.

Eduardo could see that Sal was enticed by the un-ashamed bearing of his — Eduardo's — body. He had no modesty; Sal's full disclosure of his H.I.V. was also permission to act as salaciously, as luridly as he wanted. He manifested his need in a barely conscious wriggling. His impatience made itself known in the tapping of the foot that he had placed upon Sal's abdomen. *Drink me in, Sal,* he thought. *The dark tufts of hair in my armpits, the flush pink of my aureoles. How hard, how thick are my nipples, without being touched, licked, bitten!* He watched Sal, stock-still, as he itemized his new lover's body. *Can he smell my scent of fresh soap and Kona java and sweat? Does he see how I squirm when he runs his finger between the crest of my thigh and my tight clenched balls?*

Eduardo's palpable excitement touched Sal, made him laugh, feel buoyant — almost as much as Sal's sharp yet brief realization that he was responding in kind, without fears, and without a thought about Randy. So he said to Eduardo again: "I'm looking at *you*."

"You've had months to look." Eduardo reached out for Sal's jeans, into his pocket for the condom, and tore open the packet. He got up on the bed — they were both on their knees — and placed the rubber in his mouth before expertly going down on Sal's cock, rolling the Trojan along the length of his shaft. When the condom was firmly on, he rose up and looked in Sal's eyes. "Months," he said, "months and months," before lolling backwards onto the mattress.

Sal hovered over Eduardo, placed his hands on the headboard. He dug the balls of his feet into the mattress for traction, and tilted forward to find his balance. He ran his thumb down the crack of Eduardo's ass, between it, finding the pulse there, the center, before tilting himself forward to guide his dick inside. Resting himself there a moment, letting his lover acclimate to what was about to happen, he saw Eduardo look up, bemused, before gasping with a sharp, shallow intake of air.

And then he was inside him. There was pain at first — there always was — but it was fleeting, fleeting, followed by a gentle relief and an overwhelming fulfillment. Isn't this what Eduardo had wanted — not the fucking, not the mechanics, but the intimacy? Now that they were here, that he could feel Sal full within him, his pelvis pressed close against Eduardo's thighs, his short thrusts and steady rocking against the headboard — wasn't it easy? Wasn't it? Well maybe. And maybe not. Those months of pretending. The crush of disappointment. Wondering if Sal wasn't interested. Or if he'd been damaged by his past. Or what, exactly, kept him from this, this intensity, this bliss, where each thrust was met with the controlled response of Eduardo's muscles, the warmth of his desire to pull Sal in, further in.

Jesus Christ, Sal thought. *Jesus Christ. What is he doing with his ass? Jesus Christ!* But he didn't get much further than that; instead, he fucked him faster, banging his own knuckles against the wall, thinking of how much fun he was going to have making a mess of that immaculate room.

Eduardo grabbed Sal by the hips — the faster Sal retracted, the harder he pulled him back inside. He pressed his ass hard up against Sal's pelvis, writhed there on the shaft of his cock, clenching, releasing, reinforcing: *I want this, I want this, I want this.* And Sal must have, too, because he stopped plunging, content to give Eduardo control while Sal pumped Eduardo's straining prick in his tight fist, until they both came — Eduardo first, furiously, so much cum that Sal thought it might never end, and then Sal soon after, when the contractions of Eduardo's climax were just beginning to taper.

Sal collapsed next to him. The quiet in the room was jarring, as it must have been to Celeste, whom they could hear applauding downstairs. Eduardo took the edge of the comforter and wrapped them in it, inching closer to Sal, who was gazing at the ceiling in a glassy-eyed reverie. Imelda was sniffing Sal's hand, still sticky with Eduardo's semen. He opened his palm for her to lick it. "Look," he said, propping Eduardo up on his chest to see. "I told you I could get her to come to me."

Patchwork
Part Three; Chapter Three

WAS IT POSSIBLE to get lost outside the Pacific Design Center? Sal didn't think it was, but here they were — he and Eduardo — trying to find an entrance to a Museum of Contemporary Art satellite gallery. It had to be near. The Center itself, with its geometric swaths of reflective aquamarine glass, was a less than a compelling landmark.

"What an eyesore," he said to Eduardo.

And they wandered, his boyfriend's small warm hand hooked through Sal's arm, fingertips resting on Sal's furry forearm. Sal was nearly a foot taller than Eduardo, more slender. When Sal glimpsed their silhouette as they passed a dark window, he noted the strange posture of the two of them together, the imbalance of their figures. It nagged at him, this visual. He'd seen this posture before, but where — and who it was — momentarily escaped his recollection.

When they found the MoCa entrance, he wondered why they'd passed by it not once, but twice. It was well marked and lighted, with its distinctive logo in its elegant post-modern black lettering. Perhaps they were both distracted by more immediate concerns. Sal absolutely was. He wondered, delightfully, what Eduardo — who loved to surprise him with sex in public spaces — had in store for him today.

"Finally," Eduardo said when they found the entrance. The enthusiasm in his voice turned Sal on.

As they approached the admission desk, Sal reached for his wallet — the kind attached to a dangling hip chain that fastened to a belt loop. This was a hot trend for the Westide wiggas — 'white niggers' — who played at gangsta culture. It had also found its way to the WeHo hip-hop pretenders, or giggas — 'gay niggers' — as Sal called them. He wasn't beholden to pop fashion, but he loved the heavy hang of the thick silver chain, how it reminded him of the old Chicago leather bars he had frequented to enjoy the spectacle of the butch drag.

He was pulling a twenty from his wallet when Eduardo stopped him. "I've got this," Eduardo said, flashing a membership card at the attendant.

"If you're a patron," Sal said, "why didn't you know where the entrance was?"

"And deprive myself of an elegant promenade to show you off to our community?" He sported a sly smile. A hint of a blush crossed his cheeks. "Besides, I've only been to the gallery downtown."

"So am I to understand that you're parading me around like a cheap piece of meat?"

"Cheap?" he considered, furrowing his brow in mock thought. "Not cheap, no. But a piece of meat? Absolutely."

"That," Sal laughed, then bent down to kiss him on the top of his head, "was an expert answer."

It was the weekend of their first anniversary, or as near to it as Eduardo believed. He wasn't certain what constituted a gay anniversary or, at least, their own anniversary. Was it when they had met? Their first date? That night — after those three arduous months — when they finally fucked? Or was it when Sal asked him to live with him? Eduardo had finally, recently moved into the apartment after a month-long internal debate to determine if he was ready. It wasn't that he hadn't wanted to, far from it, but he had the sneaking suspicion that Sal's request was more for convenience than anything else. Sal's sexual appetite was more than voracious. To say they were inseparable was no empty boast. Sal was on him — *in* him — with a near-religious intensity that he took not only as a dare but met with a pliant willingness to do anything, anywhere, any time. It got to the point where Sal, at first the more forceful instigator of the two, let Eduardo impose his seemingly limitless imagination on their sex life. So he figured Sal wanted them to live together to give freer reign to these impulses, to have Eduardo near at hand whenever, wherever he wanted, to do, well, whatever. As their physical life was the focal point of their relationship, Eduardo had decided that their anniversary was one year from that night last June when Sal fucked him. "Here," he said, handing Sal a brochure as they entered the gallery.

"Not another handout with sex tips," Sal kidded, taking the leaflet.

"Honey," Eduardo admonished with a sweet, shy inflection. "Why would I give you a paltry *pamphlet* when we both know I wrote the fucking book?"

"The Fucking Book," Sal said before applauding. "Author! Author!"

"And you, my biggest, my most, my most...," he searched for the right word, "insatiable fan."

"Will we be researching a new chapter today?" Sal asked. He practically licked his lips until he saw the playful look disappear from Eduardo's face. He'd been so cagey all week about coming to the gallery that Sal just assumed it was for a public display of, um, affection, not to stare at works of — what does this brochure say — *Gay Tableaux at the End of the Millennium*. When he saw the first piece in the carefully lighted, intimate anteroom — a textured Mapplethorpe calla lily with its powerfully mocking phallic stamen — he couldn't help but trail Eduardo, stare at his fine full ass, and mutter under his breath.

"Fuck art, let's fuck."

For the past year, Sal had been in what he had come to call a 'sex fog'. Admittedly his behavior had been sophomoric. He was obsessed with Eduardo, his taste, his scents, those sharp, guttural moans — far below his normal speaking voice — that mirrored, in exact syncopation, the stuttering spurt of his ejaculations. He couldn't get enough of his new lover's body, or the strange disconnect of his personality. He was intrigued by Eduardo's long stretches of a Zen-like silence followed by equally intense physical marathons. And though he loved his constant, affirmative tumescence in Eduardo's presence, he wasn't sure if he loved him the way he had Randy, unconditionally true though always difficult.

But, oh, how Eduardo brought him close again to the idea of love. How that manifested in a healthier appetite for everything in Sal's life. If he could get his head out of the "sex fog", he might think he was on the verge of that old crock, the mid-life crisis. But Sal barely considered age except in the negative contours of AIDS. *Mid-life?* Even with the new drugs he'd be lucky to live to sixty, let alone eighty. All he knew was that here was a man he wanted, desired with such compulsion that he hardly thought of the inevitable end, only what it meant to feel alive.

"Why do I want to look at the shriveled cocks of old men?" Eduardo asked in front of a painting by Gilbert & George.

"Is that a rhetorical question?"

"Don't be so sensitive, Sal. No one could ever think of your cock as 'shriveled.'" He tapped him lightly on the back of his hand like a parent admonishing a naughty child. "But is it art?"

After forty-five minutes in the gallery, Eduardo felt he had less of an idea of what constituted 'art', in general, and 'gay art', specifically, than before he'd arrived. Despite his membership, he'd only been to the downtown home of MoCa once.

"Is this all we are?" he asked Sal, as they passed erotic pencil studies, then representational paintings of phallic objects, then photos of glistening torsos, not to mention Tom of Finland's absurdly hung leathermen, Keith Haring's childlike outlines of eroticized infants, and one bullwhip up the ass photo. "Are we *nothing* but flesh?" He didn't really expect an answer, but wanted one, or at least an attempt at one.

All Sal could muster was a dismissive grunt.

Eduardo wasn't sure why the exhibition bothered him that much. Maybe he thought that surrounding themselves with some type of culture might lead to conversation, open up avenues of discussion between them that they usually surpassed in lieu of their more primal natures. But it backfired. He hadn't thought the MOCA exhibit would be so cock-centric. *Where are the dyke artists?* he thought, not that he really cared about them. Still, shouldn't they get at least one measly wall? Or was it too much to want a political perspective, especially now when — *when what?* When he had a personal link to the AIDS crisis? Was it still a crisis? You didn't see as much about it in the papers anymore.

But that wasn't foremost on his mind, either. *Please!* he thought. *You love a good dick picture as much as the next gay guy.* He laughed, since the next gay guy was Sal, who didn't seem to mind the exhibit in the least, patiently reading the placards beneath each piece. *Right! He's probably wondering if we're going to fuck in the bathroom.* It struck Eduardo as they left the current room to enter the last exhibition space that he couldn't care less if the "gay community" was depicted in such a limited light because he felt, for the moment, that this representation was true about him. He'd let sex dictate his relationship with Sal when he'd wanted much, much more. And the most lamentable thing was that he had no one to blame. He'd painted himself — that's right, *painted himself* — into this highly pleasurable, monotonous corner.

The last space in the exhibition was a single room that didn't open up from a hallway as the other galleries did, but was accessible only by door, and then with the guidance of a doorman — a serious-looking fellow in a white lab coat. As they approached him he nodded, grabbing the brass handle of the entryway with the sharp echoing squeal of rubber gloves against metal. Once enclosed in the mute, low-lit space — taking a moment for their eyes to adjust — they found that they were alone.

The long space seemed empty. The walls, what they could see of them, were the standard white. Yet as their vision altered to the abrupt shift in the level of light, each of them noticed different aspects of the room, reliant now on senses other than strict sight.

Eduardo could smell the acrid fumes of recent paint. The walls had been refinished for this show. He could see now that they were not the calm gallery white of most museums, but done in a harsher, clinical gloss.

Sal felt a soft substance underfoot as they moved further into the room. The hardwood floors had been replaced by a pliable, almost spongy mat that rendered surface noise nearly inaudible. The deliberate quiet allowed him to hear the frequency of white noise in the gallery.

The light — what little there was — originated from halogen spots in the ceiling, all of them funneled to the far wall, which is what Sal and Eduardo walked towards, cautiously, respectful of the odd serenity of the space, and their introduction into it, their sudden existence within it.

As they moved closer to that far wall, they saw that there were figures faint and hardly noticeable — gray and fading — etched into alabaster.

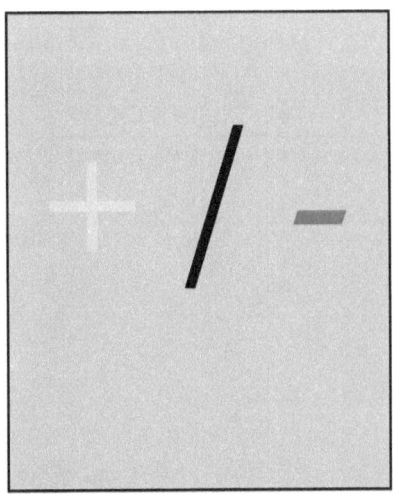

Eduardo looked at the symbols, the soft harmony of weak neutrals. He felt warmth — almost gratitude — for the simplicity of the piece. "Such a lovely balance," he said, moving closer to Sal. Then he noticed the hard black mark that kept the objects — plus, minus — forever separated.

Sal ignored the artwork's minimalist intent of sero-positive/negative couples. The figures were kept at bay with an imbalanced slash. He considered instead a broader meaning, one that wasn't related to AIDS at all. He thought of how the clash of polarities produced not only dissonance, yes, but also — and he was thinking of himself and Eduardo now as the Filipino tugged at his side to leave — how such matter could rally to create the most unavoidable, magnetic energy.

Patchwork
Part Three; Chapter Four

July 1, 1999

Dear Ben and Barbara,

How do I start this? I've written and ripped up this letter three times, each attempt more muddled than the last, too overreaching, too formal, too 'literary' to finally say the one simple thing that has caused me to write.

But first: it's hard to believe it's been a decade since the last time I saw you that day in Iowa, Ben, unloading the last of Randy's things from that humid, rented van; and we stood together, Barbara, at the peak of the Waterloo cemetery near his headstone. Do you remember the defacement of it — that ugly, intolerant graffiti? Have there been other incidents since then?

I hope not.

So, a decade has passed — a remarkable one when I stop to think about it. Within five years having H.I.V. went from certain death to a manageable condition. Amazing, right? Bittersweet, too. All those people, those men — Randy — on the wrong side of the cusp, and the rest of us negotiating what this 'reprieve' could mean. I'm truly glad to be here trying to figure it out, but I still don't trust it — this thing, this 'future'. I saw death too closely, too intimately — Randy's, true, but also — in my mind — my own. This sense of well being could easily be a trap waiting for its opportunity to strike. The drugs could fail; the virus mutate.

Yet here I am, living — and that's the word, living — in Los Angeles of all places. But what a paradox: I'd left the Midwest to survive without the weight of memory, and also — like a dog — to find a place to die. I thought L.A. would be my own cool corner beneath the front porch where I could curl up and disappear. What is that old saw about how to get God to laugh?

Oh, right. Make some plans!

I was at a gallery here recently, and saw a couple that walked its space much the same way you both did all those years ago at Navy Pier. I remember thinking — at the time, and even now — what tenderness existed between you; how Barbara's hand rested so lightly in the crook of your arm, Ben. I wondered how you could even feel her touch. But of course you could, you did, you do. However long I tried to deny him, this is how I sense Randy now: at my side, his touch light but always felt.

I wanted to send you this long overdue message of thanks; for that image of warmth, certainly, but moreover, most importantly, and without end, for your son.

Yours,
Sal

IMELDA WAS BARKING wildly, though Sal wasn't sure at what until he noticed a faint tapping at the front door. Why didn't whoever it was just use the doorbell?

"Imelda, *ihinto*," he said, one of the words he'd learned in Tagalog since the dog responded best in her master's native tongue. "Stop!" But she scratched at the door to warn against the sensed presence behind it the way she did whether someone was there or just passing in the hallway. "Move, Imelda," he yelled. The dog had thrown herself, whimpering, between him and the door. *"Lumipat!"*

Looking through the viewfinder he saw an older woman, her back a bit hunched, an overnight case at her side. "Yes," he said, opening the door. He smiled at the woman solicitously — stealing up for the inevitable sales pitch to come — when he noticed the expectant fierceness of her eyes. He knew her.

"Barbara?"

"Why not you?" she said, and slapped him across the face.

Sal was stunned. Imelda — retreating behind Sal — stopped yelping.

"There," Barbara said, retrieving her luggage, stepping into the apartment. "Now that that's over with, get me a drink."

Had he heard her correctly? *'Why not you?'* she had said, but what the hell did she mean? *I should have just smacked her back*, he thought, but the moment was gone. She was moving into the hallway, towards the kitchen, placing her purse on the kitchen table before leaning her vertical case against the lower cupboards. *Is she planning on staying awhile?* he thought. *Here?* But his attention was drawn towards the open door, expecting the arrival of her husband.

"He's not coming," she said, watching Sal as he peered into the hallway. "He's dead."

She didn't say it with malice; nor with delight; nor regret. Her tone was neutral, as clear as a fact she'd long gotten used to, and Sal found himself infused with a melancholy sharpened by his deduction that Ben must have been dead for quite some time.

"Of course I'll tell you all about it," she said from the alcove table where she sat, watching the process of Sal's features coming to terms with the idea of Ben's death. "In good time, yes. But that drink first."

In the kitchen, Sal pulled a tumbler from a cabinet, grabbed ice from the freezer, and rummaged through what few liquor bottles they had. He clutched a hardly touched Dewar's and pulled two shots from the bottle, which met with a sigh of approval from his unexpected guest.

She knocked half its contents back almost as soon as he'd handed the glass to her. She licked her lips to prolong the sweet sting of the Scotch, then downed the rest of the liquid, handing the empty glass to him. "Another, barkeep, but this time join an old woman in her afternoon reveries."

"Barbara," he said, in equal parts amazement, for how summarily she finished the Dewar's – and confusion – for her presence at all in his apartment. "What the hell are you doing here?"

"What do you think?" Barbara asked. There was petulance in her voice, and perhaps a bit of posturing. She had considered the question herself while she threw together her clothes and toiletries back in Iowa. She had thought about it again on the nerve-wracking flight to California, but she was distracted, as all first time fliers are, with the novel sounds of the cabin, each creak a possible harbinger of disaster, each bump a certain indication of the onslaught of certain death (though once on the ground she realized the flight had been as smooth and controlled as possible). When she landed, her nerves were frayed, and the question why — why was she flying halfway across the country to see her son's widowed lover? — was no closer to clarity than when she had spontaneously booked the flight after reading and re-reading his unanticipated letter. "Have a drink with me," she goaded, buying more time to ponder the question.

"Another Scotch?"

"Yes," she said, "but don't be so stingy."

He returned with a full tumbler for her and a tea glass of water with crushed ice for him. "Vodka?" she asked.

"Nope," Sal said as he sat at the small alcove table across from her. He watched her sip her drink, more slowly now, her harried energy waning. "Just water. I indulge a different sort of cocktail now." Though Sal found Barbara elegantly put together in a tan pantsuit set off by a sumptuous burgundy scarf, her face looked depleted — a cheerless, age-spotted facsimile of its former self. Her hair had thinned since the last time he saw her; those thick gray strands were now brittle and teased into place. He imagined her on a reconnaissance mission in the airport bathroom with just water and her spindly fingers trying desperately to mold the fragile tresses into shape. For a moment, she seemed to him lost.

"What kind of cocktails?" she asked. "Protease? A transcriptase with a side of Zithromax?"

He was impressed, but said, "Stop showing off."

"I had a lot of time to read." She let the statement hang there. As she sat and scratched the head of Imelda — who had at first hid under the table until she had slowly made herself submissive at Barbara's side — Sal knew no other information would be, for the moment, forthcoming. "She's a sweet dog. When did you get her?"

Now it was Sal's turn to be evasive. "She belongs to a friend."

"Friend?" She raised her eyebrows, informing Sal that she knew the word had other connotations.

"Yes," he said, wondering what she might make of Eduardo; and what would Eduardo think of this sudden figure from Sal's past that had — so promptly! — ingratiated herself with his troublesome dog. Sal checked to see if Imelda was licking Barbara's hand, if she had possibly coerced the dog with the damp promise of Scotch on her fingertips.

Barbara rubbed the nub of Imelda's scalp — touching the soft dander on her head with the gentlest pressure. The animal had such a calming authority on her. "It's been quite some time," she said to Sal. After being trapped inside the cramped space of the airplane, and then in the humid, narrow backseat of what must have been the slowest cab in the world, it was a relief to be sitting still, going nowhere, with no other immediate connection to make. The booze didn't hurt, either. "You look good. Healthy."

"I am. I'm both. Good. And healthy." How bizarre — Barbara here, petting the dog, as if she'd popped by for a brief chat. And that damn Imelda. *What a little traitor!* "Is that why you're here? To make sure I'm okay? I couldn't be better."

"This *'reprieve'* you wrote of," she said. "I had to see if for myself." She finished her second drink and laughed: high-pitched, staccato, on the verge of hysteria. But the sound was not the cackle of an old crone; there was a girlish note in her voice, innocent and freeing. "Not only do you live," she said. "You *thrive*. And the truth is, the truth—" She didn't laugh this time; she jeered. "The bitter truth is, oh, I don't fucking know. Why my son? Why Ben? Why not you?"

There it was, her phrase again, and there was no mistaking her meaning. He should have died; not Randy.

She stopped to gaze at Sal — her weary eyes both indifferent and penetrating — before she said, with an accumulated self-pity that staggered both of them, "Why not me?"

Her outburst exhausted her. She asked Sal if it would bother him if she took a short catnap on his fine, modern sofa. But before he could answer she'd gotten up shakily, then walked with such consciously controlled effort to the living room that he didn't have the heart to tell her no.

Eduardo arrived home in the early evening cradling a bag of groceries in his arms. "Who is that?" he asked of the prone figure on the sofa. From where he stood, he could only see the top of a head and the sleeping body of his dog. "Why is Imelda sleeping at their feet?"

"That's my mother-in-law," Sal answered.

"My mother?!" Eduardo screamed. *"Ina!* My *Ina?* What is she doing here?"

"Not your mother, Eduardo. Randy's mother."

"Randy's mother?" Eduardo knew little about Randy, and nothing of his family.

Sal reached out to touch Eduardo's face; his cheeks were red with confusion. "Yes. Randy's mother."

"But, but—"

"My thoughts exactly."

"Imelda," Eduardo demanded, still holding the groceries to his chest. *"Pababa.* Get down right now."

The dog stirred, jumped over the light cover Sal had placed on Barbara, but remained on the sofa.

"Right now!" Eduardo repeated. "Or no *kainan* tonight."

Barbara felt a motion over her body. She shot up — disoriented by the sofa, the dog, the apartment. She saw Sal and remembered she was in Los Angeles. Then she noticed the short Asian man at his side, the paper bag in his arms. "Did I sleep that long?" she said, getting up and moving towards her purse on the alcove table. She rifled through it for some crumpled bills, and handed the money to Eduardo.

"What's this for?" he asked.

"Dinner."

Eduardo scowled. "You think I'm the delivery boy?"

"Barbara," Sal said, retrieving the money from Eduardo's tight grasp and putting it back into her hands. "This is my friend, Eduardo."

"Forgive me," she said to Eduardo, blushing. She extended her hand to him, the one still holding the cash. "I've no idea what I was thinking. I'm so disoriented."

Eduardo stared down at her hand, the wad of cash still in her grip. He had to admit that the situation was ludicrous, and would have easily conceded the folly of an old woman, but he got the distinct impression that she was now enjoying her mistake at his expense — she kept pressing the cash against his arm though it was clear he did not have food.

"Listen," Sal said to her, moving her away from Eduardo. "Clean yourself up. We'll take you to Hollywood for dinner."

"We're taking her out to dinner?" Eduardo asked as soon as she had retreated to the bathroom. "Why?"

"Because all she's had to eat today," Sal said, "is Scotch."

"Still." Eduardo went to retrieve Imelda, who had nestled in the light throw Barbara had folded and placed on the sofa before she went to the bathroom. Under his breath he admonished the dog in Tagalog, then kissed her on the nose. "What does she want?" he asked Sal.

"I'm not sure." Sal was peeved at his boyfriend's lack of generosity given the circumstances. "Perhaps she wants a bit of bread, some protein, a dry Merlot."

"That's not what I mean."

"I know. But it's not like she just popped over from Brentwood. She flew in from Iowa. I don't know why. She doesn't seem to know why, either — though I find that hard to believe." He took the blanket from the sofa and put it back in the foot-drawer where he'd taken it from earlier. "Still, we can try to be accommodating. She seems in need of a little kindness."

"Gentlemen." Barbara had reentered the room, refreshed and with a renewed sprightliness to her step.

Neither Sal nor Eduardo knew if she had heard any of their conversation.

"Let me treat you to dinner," she said. "Your choice. Anywhere. But I have only one request." She stared at Eduardo. "No Chinese."

Though Eduardo had a car it was a small black Miata, a used two-seater he'd driven to L.A. from Michigan. So Sal called a cab which took 40 minutes to arrive, and they all piled into the backseat, Barbara insisting she sit between them — ostensibly for Sal and Eduardo's comfort, though Eduardo felt it was more to keep him and Sal apart, an intuition reinforced when she slid closer to Sal's side of the cab and rested her hand, rather delicately, on his knee.

Eduardo had no idea what to make of her. He certainly wasn't offended by her misconception earlier; given his size and ethnicity, it wasn't the first time he'd been mistaken for a delivery boy. But Chinese? Please! Anyone with the slightest knowledge of Asian physiognomy could plainly see that he was — if not Filipino, then certainly not Chinese. He thought, *just look at the cab driver, lady: slight features, slit-eyes, bad pasty complexion. Obviously Mandarin. Now compare that to me — rounded features, oval eyes, smooth dark skin.* Yet it wasn't the misunderstanding that bothered him, but rather how little he knew of her, the lack of information Sal disclosed regarding his general past, and his life with Randy, specifically. He knew Sal's ex by name, and a few choice details, like the color of his hair, his eyes, his friendly disposition and bitchy wit, the way he constantly challenged Sal, kept him on his game. He also knew that Sal — though he'd never said this to Eduardo directly — still loved Randy deeply. He had pretended to move on, but Eduardo knew this was not — could not — be true. Because whatever he learned from Sal about his ex-lover was always amended in Eduardo's mind with this unspoken proviso: Randy gave me AIDS.

The Mother, to Eduardo's memory, was not even a footnote. But here she was, sitting next to Sal, hand on his knee, cooing over whatever small piece of L.A. history Sal pointed out in his role as tour guide.

"That's Pink Dot," Sal told Barbara, as if the company that delivered various sundries 24 hours a day was of particular note. "And over there," he said a few minutes later, "is the Hollywood sign, which you *might* see if it was lighter out and there wasn't so much smog."

It's not that Barbara wasn't interested — Sal was surely an inventive guide, having pointed out hotels famed for their drug-addled celebrity clientele, and the forthcoming retail spot of a porn entrepreneur — but she was hungry. There was little of that famed L.A. traffic, and yet they managed to catch nearly every red light on the boulevard. "Why are the cabbies in this town so goddamned slow?"

"L.A.'s a cab driver's purgatory," Eduardo answered.

"How so?" she asked.

"The slowest, dimmest, most sluggish are sent here in exile."

"And you have inside knowledge of this phenomenon?" she asked.

She asked it with a slight inflection in her voice that Sal knew was a setup, and tried to gesture to Eduardo not to proceed, but Eduardo ignored him.

"It's common knowledge," he said.

"And are most of them Asian?" Barbara said innocently. "I only ask because both of the drivers I've had today have been."

Eduardo was furious — not because she was an unabashed racist, but because she had a point. He looked to Sal for a way out of this dead end.

"Look," Sal said. "We're finally here."

Eduardo helped Barbara out of the cab. "Perhaps after dinner, Mrs. Manning—"

"Oh, call me Barbara, please."

"Why thank you, Barbara," he said. "Perhaps after dinner I can take you and Sal back to the apartment by rickshaw. You might like that."

Eduardo chose the restaurant, and though Barbara was clear about no Chinese food, she said nothing about any other Asian derivatives. So they were in a *shabu shabu* place off Hollywood Boulevard, huddled around tables that were also coil-heating stovetops, waiting for the water to boil.

"I have to say," Barbara said, "I don't understand the concept of going to a restaurant where you cook your own food."

"I'm not surprised," Eduardo retorted as he arranged the soy and peanut oil dishes to prepare them with scallion, daikon root, garlic. He'd chosen the place with tactical purpose — so that he and Sal could sit on one side of the square heaters; and to instill upon Barbara that forced sense of community that such dining imposed. "Breaking bread" with a stranger was one thing; cooking with them another.

Because Barbara had never had *shabu shabu*, and Sal's experience with the food was limited, it was left to Eduardo to order the general dishes, a combination of thinly sliced Kobe beef, pork, chicken, salmon, and shrimp. The waitress – a frail woman with a black bob – checked the burners. As Sal, Eduardo and Barbara talked or weathered awkward silences, the water began to heat, the stainless steel lids to shake and clatter. Steam rose up in sharp ribbons.

"If you put your face over the steam," Sal said, "you can get a facial with your meal."

"For the prices they're charging," Barbara said, "I would hope so."

Drinks arrived. The delicate Asian waitress had a bicep like a tree trunk, balancing a tray full of waters, green teas for the men, and Scotch rocks for Barbara, who took a loud sip from the rim-full glass.

"So," she asked them, "how did you two meet?"

It wasn't as much a question as a taunt; her voice was pleasant yet also mocking, and Eduardo sat ramrod straight in his chair, ready to pounce. But Sal put a firm hand on his leg beneath the table, and smiled delicately at Barbara. "If I thought you were truly interested in that, Barbara," he said, "I'd gladly share the juicy details with you."

"Juicy, eh? Such a *ripe* word." Barbara pursed her lips, thinking. The lighting in the restaurant — small halogen spots that circled each of the tables — created an enclosed space that gave a sense of seclusion to the tables. They seemed isolated from the other patrons; overly intimate with each other. "Juicier than how you met my son?"

Sal squeezed Eduardo above the knee — just slightly, just so — to indicate that he had this under control. "Did Randy tell you about that?" He couldn't have asked any more nicely, but it was a sweetness that encompassed the sting.

Eduardo thought he saw Barbara squirm, uncomfortable with Sal's question. True, he enjoyed her discomfort, and just as quickly sought to relieve her of it. It was enough to know the subject of her dead son was a sore spot for her; he didn't need her to wallow in it.

"Barbara," he said, waiting for her gaze to meet his own. "What brings you to California? I asked Sal, but he wasn't sure." Her eyes never broke contact with his while she retrieved from her purse a letter. She took it from its envelope, unfolded it (*almost lovingly*, he thought), and handed it to him.

"This," she said.

Eduardo turned the letter over in his hands, saw that it was from Sal, and even though Barbara had given it to him he looked at Sal for approval to read it. Sal nodded his consent. Yet as Eduardo scanned the words he grew uncomfortable. Even though he'd been given permission by both of them, it was as though he'd chanced upon an intimate gesture not meant for his eyes to see. And now that they were both staring at him, watching him pry into their private moment, he felt – at first – self-conscious, dirty, then privileged to read Sal's feelings about having survived with H.I.V. until, finally, he – Eduardo – seemed crossed by sadness and anger and a disbelief that Sal had displayed more vulnerability in two pages to a virtual stranger than he ever had when they were alone. Eduardo looked at Barbara – uptight in her tan suit and tragic hair – and was shocked to think he'd let himself feel threatened by this sad old woman, when the real peril, clear and precise in Sal's letter, was the past. But that was a conversation for himself and Sal, and for another time.

The food arrived — three platters of various raw meats thinly sliced and fanned around the edges, one on top of the next, like playing cards. A separate plate was filled with vegetables — broccoli, cabbage, mushrooms, onions — and piles of translucent glass noodles. *If this is what they eat in California*, Barbara thought, *no wonder they all look sick.*

Eduardo asked the waitress for a fork for Barbara, then picked up his chopsticks to demonstrate how to eat *shabu shabu* by selecting some beef and cabbage leaves to immerse in the boiling water. After thirty seconds or so he fished out the beef, which had quickly turned from its bright, marbleized red to a pinkish gray, and dipped it lightly in a Ponzu sauce he had sprinkled liberally with chopped scallions.

"I have to admit," Barbara said after doing the same thing with a choice serving of salmon, "this is damn tasty."

"Eduardo turned me on to this," Sal said.

"Of course he did."

Eduardo smiled, filling his boiling pot with other meats and veggies.

"So the letter," Sal said to Barbara, "is what motivated your trip here."

"The letter, yes." She asked the waitress for a third Scotch. "And disbelief. I think I needed to see you for myself." This she said to Sal while negotiating the slippery noodles from the water. "I didn't want to tell you about Ben in a letter."

"You could have called," Eduardo helpfully offered.

"I might have."

"What stopped you?" Sal asked.

"You mean other than the unlisted number?"

"Habit," Sal told them after they stopped laughing. "Randy always insisted on it. For someone so loose — " He stole a glance at Barbara, aware of his indelicacy, but she was gazing back at him to continue. "For someone so carefree, he really valued his . . . our privacy."

Though he'd wanted to know more about Randy, to get Sal to talk about his past in order to disseminate it, Eduardo didn't want that information to come to him now, with Barbara here. He changed the subject.

"What about your husband, Ben?" Eduardo asked.

"Ah Ben," she said, her voice trailing off. "I guess I've tantalized and withheld that particular story long enough. But it's simple, really. Our son died. My husband never recovered from the loss. He let himself go — wasted away in front of my eyes." It was Barbara's moment of indelicacy; she looked over at Sal just in time to see him avert his eyes from the table. "Wouldn't eat. Couldn't sleep. I came home from the market one Saturday — not 'one' Saturday, the Saturday, nearly two years to the day of Randy's death — and there was Ben, slumped forward on the desk in his study." She paused, sipping from an empty glass of Scotch. "When I feel forgiving and poetic I tell people he died of a broken heart."

"I can only—" Sal began, but stopped himself from adding the word 'imagine', because it was a lie. He didn't need to range through his mind to understand the concept of dying from a broken heart. He knew the crushing reality of it. He struggled, those first few years after Randy's demise, to not fall victim to the debilitation of grief. Sal reached out to Eduardo, seeking his hand beneath the table, entwining their fingers together. "I know how Ben must have felt."

"You should," Barbara said, her voice clear, compassionate.

This is what binds us, Sal thought of Barbara, and, surprisingly, of Eduardo also, *loss*.

"But I don't know what he felt," she said. "In the end I didn't understand him any more than I did my son. After Randy died — after the arrangements and the funeral; all the sympathetic stares from neighbors, strangers; long after a sensible period of bereavement was over — after all that, Ben was still, oh, I don't know."

"Absent?" Eduardo said. He was stroking the top of Sal's hand. His own past was littered with brief – what? Relationships? No. More like trial runs towards something, someone more permanent. He wanted to believe Sal could be that someone, but he was uncertain.

"Not absent, Eduardo," Sal said, because — though he wasn't there, hadn't seen Ben, hadn't bothered to do as much as call them out of courtesy — he knew. "Distant."

"Distant," Barbara repeated. "Thank you, yes. But also expectant. He was always waiting, sitting in that damn moldy study, pictures of Randy embalmed — right, that's the word — embalmed beneath that Plexiglas desktop. Staring intently through half open curtains."

"He was on sentry," Sal said. He could still see that room, feel its oppressive humidity, smell that sweet aroma of stale cigars which was bizarre since he knew that Ben didn't smoke.

Barbara and Eduardo looked at Sal, puzzled.

"He was waiting for Randy to come home," Sal clarified.

"He was," Barbara confirmed, reaching once again into her purse. She handed something to Sal wrapped in an onion paper that crinkled as he opened it: the photo of Randy — nine years old, gap-tooted, grinning — that he and Ben had marveled at all those years ago in that dim study. "When he was lucid, those precious few times when I could engage him, he would tap his finger on his desk just above that photo and say, 'Sal loved this picture.' That was it. 'Sal loved this picture.'" Barbara laughed, the reminiscence fresh to her, poignant still. "One afternoon, late winter, the sun setting outside his window — such a gorgeous sunset, Sal, you would have loved it — he did

153

it again: touched the photo, said those words, gazed with such ache out at those empty plains. And it was clear to me that he wasn't looking for, or even remembering, our son. He was waiting for you."

Patchwork

Part Three; Chapter Six

BARBARA AND SAL roamed the concrete slabs in front of Graumann's Chinese Theatre. There was the imprint of Marilyn Monroe — her tiny stiletto heels a spiky exclamation point to the depth of her narrow foot. There was Clark Gable, his mark deep and masculine, his name etched in the stone with finesse.

"I have so many regrets," Barbara confided in Sal. "All of them worthless."

Sal didn't respond, just stayed by her side in the theatre's courtyard. Graumann's had undergone recent upgrades. There'd been reports in the *L.A. Times* of a new planned complex that would transform the seedy glamour of Old Hollywood, which Sal loved, into the new Times Square of the West. The Disney-fied version. He rued these coming changes. "Regrets are like potato chips," he told her in his warmest, most sage voice. "You can't have just one."

"That's so stupid," she said, "I could almost laugh."

"What's stopping you?"

"Self-respect."

Superheroes — Batman! Spiderman! Zorro! — shared the sidewalk with camera-toting tourists. The homeless panhandled from executives chatting on their cell phones. "Yo, boss, help a brother out!" Vendors peddled

Star Maps, cinnamon-sweet *churros*, incense. Sal loved watching the hustlers here — the Vietnam vet pitching quarters; the leathery drug dealer, in old polyester flares, shuffling past preppy college kids with a whispered litany of temptations: "smoke, X, crack-cocaine"; the young girls of L.A., barely in their teens, dressed in the hoochie skank finery of the latest pop idols. He thrilled to this immediacy as much as he loved his distance from it, acknowledging to himself that his removal from youth culture was another step, as he neared 50, in the widening gap of his middle age.

Yes!

"What do you think of Eduardo?" he asked as they strolled the boulevard. He needed to clarify to Barbara that he wasn't seeking approval or validation. He wanted her opinion of Eduardo because, after the last year, he still found him maddeningly elusive. Warm, yes. Receptive and loving, too. Yet also imbued with a strange formality that bordered on the secretive. Barbara had not responded, so he asked her again. "What do you think of him?"

Having spent the last week with them, she knew where Sal's line of inquiry was headed. "He's waiting on your lead."

"My lead?"

"Don't be coy, Sal." She knelt on the sidewalk to touch the raised, gilded letters of Dizzy Gillespie's name. He'd been one of Ben's favorite musicians.

"I really don't know what you mean," Sal said.

"Of course you do." Her tone was short. She wanted to enjoy the memory of Ben in happier times, listening to jazzy riffs of joy and wonder and, sometimes, the melancholy notes beneath the melody. Her conversation with Sal was like that — pleasant on the surface, churning underneath. Was it possible that Sal was asking Barbara for permission to love again? "Eduardo watches. He's like one of those gentleman callers, waiting to declare his intentions." The lettering of Gillespie's name was cold to the touch, comforting. "But he wants to be certain first."

Certain of what? Sal wanted to ask. But he knew Eduardo never made a move without calibrating the response first. This had happened with the sex. It happened again after their dinner of *shabu shabu*. Cuddled in bed, without instigation or even the simplest of segues, Eduardo had asked Sal if he loved him. Sal knew that telling him 'no', that he wasn't sure, wouldn't be good enough. He deflected the question with another. "Do you love me?"

Eduardo didn't answer, just held him as if the answer might be 'yes'. "I'm glad she's here," he said, pointing towards the other room.

"Truly, Eduardo. You don't have to exaggerate."

"I didn't say I liked her." He ran his fingertips across Sal's skin, distracted by the soft chest hair that recently started to gray. "But she's strong. She doesn't mince words. And she has a strange effect on you."

"On me?" Sal laughed.

There was no rancor in Eduardo's soft voice when he spoke, just a touch of sadness. "You can't be evasive with her the way you are with me. She doesn't let you retreat."

"What are you talking about?" Sal asked. He wondered if Eduardo knew that his description of Barbara was also, greatly, evocative of her son.

"I can't compete with him," Eduardo said.

No, Sal thought. *You can't. I don't want you to.*

157

"It's an unfair advantage, Sal. I can't measure up to a memory."

"You don't have to," Sal reassured him, leaning in for a kiss.

Eduardo turned away.

"No," he said, "I don't."

In her few weeks in L.A. Barbara had been with Sal to many neighborhoods: Beverly Hills, Chinatown, Silverlake, Bel Air. No area seemed more prevalent or important than another, each a continuum of the grand L.A. sprawl. She noticed that nestled among the isolated grandeur of Beverly Hills was the echo of thrift-store chic imported — and vastly marked-up — from Silverlake. The immigrant enclave of Echo Park bled into Benedict Canyon as maids, nannies, gardeners. He drove her from place to place. They traveled in comfortable silence. She caught her reflection in store windows, polished cars. She was smiling or, at least, not scowling. She felt happy for the first time in a long while. Yet when she contemplated her new mood she had to admit that maybe it was just temporary relief from years of solitude, an isolation she'd imposed on herself after first Randy, then her husband, died. Room to grieve, she'd told herself. But Sal had never fully mourned Randy. He ran.

"You know I'm leaving tomorrow," she said as they continued down the Walk of Fame.

He was surprised; she'd not mentioned it before. "I thought you had an open-ended ticket."

"Did I say that?" Barbara couldn't recall.

"No," he admitted. "I just thought."

"That's sweet of you," she said. "To assume."

"I didn't —," he stumbled.

"I didn't think you were asking me to stay."

"Of course not," he said, too quickly. "Though I'm amazed I haven't asked you to leave."

"As am I," she conceded. "Why haven't you?"

"I'm not sure."

"I am."

"Oh no," Sal slurred, deliberate and queenly; his voice a pinched of over-elaborated sibilance. "Is this like that part of the movie where the surprise visitor reveals their philanthropic intentions, and a lesson is learned by all?"

"Hardly."

"I'm warning you, Barbara," he said, his voice play-ful, "if you turn into a wise and kindly old black woman on me then I'll have no choice but to become tragic."

"What makes you think you aren't tragic now?" She wondered if she was joking with him. He had told her that he'd had no intention of remaining in L.A., but here he was. Nine years was a long time to consider temporary. And Eduardo? Was he fleeting for Sal? She had little feel-ing for Eduardo, but thinking of him in this light brought her to Randy. If he had lived *(if only he had lived)* would he and Sal still be together? She wanted to believe they would be, though she had no way of knowing.

They walked east on Hollywood Boulevard, past more and more names, until they came to stand near the edge of Rock Hudson's fading star. Sal thought of Randy at that moment, how could he not? *How apropos*, he thought. When he and Randy had watched the press announcement confirming, after months of speculation, that Hudson was stricken with AIDS, Randy's mocking rancor unnerved Sal. "America's 'man's man'," Randy kept repeating, a phrase from the newscast. The cruel tone of Randy's voice underscored their shared frustrations, their unspoken — though always close — feelings of injustice. *Perhaps now,* they thought, but could not say, *perhaps now we can hope.*

"Do you ever think of him?" Barbara asked.

"Rock Hudson?" Sal said.

"No, Randy."

"Of course I think of him," he said to Barbara. "But I try not to."

"You must," she said, though she herself imagined the strapping frame of the handsome dead actor and not her son. "If you don't, you'll never let him go."

"You see," he said, his eyes welling, then overflowing, with tears. They felt warm, perfect on his dry skin. "You see," he repeated. "Tragic!"

Barbara let him cry. She didn't move to embrace him. People passed them on the boulevard — a few visibly annoyed that they were hogging the prime space of such an infamous star — Rock Hudson, the human face of AIDS! Yet she quietly refused to budge.

A young Goth punk — her legs slashed with the strings of tattered fishnets, her torso costumed in heavy black fabrics that were too warm for the time of year — stepped out from the small crowd that had gathered. She put her arms around Sal. He was surprised, yes, and touched, too. He was also offended. He could fuck a stranger without a second thought. But share a meaningful embrace? He gazed down at her. She hugged him at the waist. He tried to make eye contact. He couldn't get past the mesmerizing blood red eye shadow fanning along the flesh from the inner eye to a severe point at her temples. He thought she might smell rank — as musty, perhaps, as the concept of Goth in the nineties itself — but she didn't. Beneath the death mask, she radiated sweetness. She smelled like lush ripe fruit. Mangoes.

"I miss him, too," the Goth said, her voice smoky as a seductress. "Such a public sorrow."

And then she was gone.

He felt himself being led away by Barbara. She had taken hold of his arm and was guiding him back to Highland Avenue, retracing their steps.

"Why is it," she asked him, "that the two of us are always surrounded by the dead?"

Eduardo made coffee. Cup after cup of it. No one ordered coffee straight. His nostrils stung with its bitter aroma. Peaberry. French fucking roast. Decaf non-fat this. Double-shot no foam that. It was L.A. There had to be a personal stamp. *Macchiato* with lime rind. Espresso glazed with chocolate shavings. For Tiffany spelled with a 'ph.'

Tiphany!

He went on autopilot; he did every day now. He used to love this job — the mindless work of a barista. It made no claims. It paid the rent, just barely. It kept him occupied. Invisible.

But Sal saw him. At least, he had once. Thousands of men had walked through this door on Sunset. They grabbed their *lattes*, their *frappuccinos*. They left.

Sal had lingered. Why? He listened, interested and aloof. Played it cool. Emanated warmth. He asked the boy who made his coffee to step out from the counter and show him who he was.

I'm nobody, Eduardo indicated. *I'm not like these phonies.* But his integrity, his modesty, was as false as L.A.'s star-fucker bravado. He knew Sal had waited for him to reveal himself. He had never pressured him.

So he receded. Relaxed into it. When Barbara showed up, Eduardo understood there was a third partner: Randy. He'd been sharing their bed all this time. *Sal will never love me.*

"Do you love me?" Sal had asked him. But when he looked into Eduardo's eyes to say it, Eduardo had seen not passion, not devotion, but such blank sweetness that all he could think was: *what difference would it make?*

"Hey, buddy," asked another in a long line of demanding customers. "Where's my pumpkin cappuccino?"

"My name's Eduardo," he said, loudly grinding beans. "And you can wait until it's damn good and ready."

Dinner again. Sal had been cooking since four. It was seven when Barbara poured herself a generous glass of *Brunello*. Sal told her it was his favorite red wine, so she picked a bottle up on their way back. Expensive, nearly forty bucks, but it was a night to celebrate. *Another ending*, she thought. *Let's drink to that.*

"How was your day?" she asked Eduardo, who had come back from work silent and, she thought, irritated.

"Uneventful,'" he said, dismissing her quickly and heading towards the kitchen to see what smelled so enticing.

"No celebrity sightings today, honey?" Sal asked Eduardo playfully. "No one desperately incognito screaming to be recognized?" Eduardo had been distant with him since Barbara had arrived, so he acted as a peacekeeper, deflecting Eduardo teasingly, biding his time until Barbara was gone. Then they could talk. He brought to the table the dishes of a traditional Filipino meal. Shrimp *Pancit* over rice noodles; *Bibingka* bread covered with thick coconut milk for sweetness; eggplant *Adobo* for both smoothness and bitterness; and Brussels sprouts, which he brought out last to remind Eduardo that he had not forgotten about him, or their first meal together. Barbara stared at the unfamiliar foods, but her week in California had softened her. Instead of resistance, she looked forward to tasting these unusual delicacies, as did Imelda, who was at her feet by the table.

Eduardo was visibly affected. First by the *Pancit*, which he hadn't had in years; then the *Bibingka*, a favorite from his childhood. Eggplant Adobo — he had to refrain from licking his lips. The aromas were rich, evocative, comforting. This was food that smelled like love.

When Sal brought the last dish and uncovered it, Eduardo froze. *Goddamned Brussels sprouts.* They had eaten them on their first date. But they were wrong for this meal — too earthy, too American, too deliberate. Sal had very consciously chosen these foods, yet where did these leafy bitter compact heads of cabbage fit in? Trying to figure out the connection between these Filipino delicacies of his childhood, his heritage, and this mass of acrid greens, Eduardo was stumped. There was no logical bond; it was all a crazy-quilt of dissonant flavors. The *Pancit*, the *Bibingka*, the *Adobo* — there was harmony. The Brussels sprouts were opposition. Was Sal telling him they were over? Was this closure? What did the fucking Brussels sprouts mean?

"Excuse me," he said, rising from the table.

"What's wrong?" Sal asked.

"Are you okay?" Barbara thought he looked pale.

"It's nothing," he said. "I've lost my appetite."

Sal was wounded. Eduardo was rejecting these dishes he'd made for him. "Sit down," he demanded, his voice harsh enough that Eduardo did as he was told.

Even Barbara was startled. She'd seen a variety of emotions pass through Sal, but each — until today — was attenuated, muted. In the short time she knew him, she'd had to learn to read the supple shapes of his feelings. But he was yelling at Eduardo. Nothing soft about that. He was confused, distressed, belligerent.

"He spent hours making this for you," she said to Eduardo.

"Don't," he said. He had clenched his hands into tight fists. "I don't want *this*," he said to her, though it was Sal he glared at, all the while point to the vegetables.

What didn't he want? Sal thought. *Greens?*

"I don't want *this*," he repeated, the sweeping gesture of his hand indicating the entire room, all that was in it. He stormed away from the table.

Sal was going to scream at Eduardo — *what do you want, motherfucker, what do you want?!* — but he didn't. He stared at the table, all the plates indigenous to Eduardo — his background, his childhood, his *essence* —

and couldn't help but see the effrontery of the Brussels sprouts, which were not about Eduardo or even about the two of them as a couple, but about Sal, his need to mark and alter everything.

He stood motionless.

Yet Barbara was on her feet, moving lithely towards her target. "Eduardo!"

"Leave me alone. Leave *us* alone."

She grabbed his arm, spun him towards her. Her strength shocked them both. "In the morning, when I leave, I'll be alone. But you," she poked his chest, then pointed her finger back at Sal to include him, "you don't have to be. You have what my son did not. You have time. You have Sal. So figure out what you want, and get on with it.

"Now sit down and eat whatever the hell this shit is."

Barbara was on the sofa bed, complete with extra throwpillows and soft blue sheets, which she laid upon without a cover to feel the cool desert air that drifted through the open windows every night. Then she waited for Imelda to pace her sleeping area until the dog, sensing her slowed breathing, jumped up to circle and settle at her feet.

Tonight Imelda came to her immediately. She was barely prone before she felt the dog's soft fur against her ankles. They'd never owned a pet, not even when Randy was a child, though she'd read that dogs were especially sensitive to human emotions. Barbara thought she and Imelda had 'bonded' — how she hated that word! — due to a combination of elements: her own initial indifference to the animal; a general sense of female solidarity; acknowledgement of the top dog in the pecking order. But now she wasn't sure. Had Imelda come to her to escape a tension in the apartment that had been there before her arrival? Was she seeking solace? An ally?

"I know, I know," she said to Imelda, reaching down to stroke her sweet spot behind the ears. "I'll miss you, too."

Eduardo lay on the edge of the bed, as far from Sal as possible. Their backs were to each other, but both knew that neither was asleep.

Eduardo tapped his fingers against the baseboard. He wanted to distract his angry thoughts, lull himself to sleep. But he was furious, pissed at his dog on the couch with that exasperating woman, pissed at that woman! He'd done a good job of disliking her all week, though tonight she surprised him. It was almost as if she cared. Mostly he was pissed at Sal — why didn't *he* come after him instead of Barbara? And how dare Sal make such a confusing and, goddamn it, delicious meal!

But Eduardo was most annoyed at himself. He'd let his own comfort with Sal, and that intoxicating rush of easily accessible sex, distract him from the greater aim. Which was? Oh, so simple, yet the hardest thing of all. To risk telling Sal how he felt — earlier in the week; earlier in the year — even if, as Eduardo suspected, the love might not be reciprocal.

Was he that insecure?

It took hours for Eduardo to nod off that night. Questions, unanswerable or perhaps best left alone, plagued his sleep.

Sal dozed off and on in the soft streetlight that filtered through their bedroom curtains. He knew Eduardo was upset with him, but still he had come to their room, to their bed. Randy would have stomped off in a snit, slammed the front door shut with such force it would rattle the walls, then he'd slink off with his frustrations to the nearest bar for a glass of beer and a speedy fuck. Though they weren't speaking, Sal felt Eduardo's warm body near him and that was comfort enough.

After 4:00 a.m., the light from the street still seeping through the bedroom blinds, Sal opened the bedside drawer — slowly, quietly, so that Eduardo would not, could not, hear it — and removed the picture of the young Randy. He ran a finger over the matte surface. He smiled happily, folded the photo back up, and slipped it back into the drawer as slowly and quietly as before. He didn't notice that — before returning Randy's fresh-faced and thoroughly lovable mug to its place of safekeeping — he whispered to him not 'goodnight', but 'goodbye.'

*   *   *

They were awkward at the airport — Sal and Barbara. He pulled her luggage. She moved slowly, almost reluctantly, Sal thought, until she said she couldn't wait to get home.

"It was good to see you," he said.

"It was good to see you." She laughed. "Hell, it was good to see anybody. Even Eduardo."

"I find that hard to believe."

"You find a lot of things hard to believe."

He knew what she meant. What he once found abrasive in her, he now thought refreshing. He'd planned on a short visit to Los Angeles; now he lived here. He thought AIDS would take him quickly, but that — so far — had not been the case.

"They're getting ready to board," she said.

"I'll walk you to the gate."

She turned to face him, placed her hand gently on his chest. "I can manage."

"That's something I do believe."

"You can bet on it," she said, removing her suitcase from his grip. She walked, the rollers squealing behind, down the long airport hallway.

"Barbara," he called after her though she did not stop. "You're welcome whenever you want."

She waved.

He would never see her again. He watched her for a moment — so determined, so alone. When he turned to leave he could still hear the squeaky wheels of her suitcase.

"Take care of yourself, Sal," she said as she moved farther down the terminal jetway. The suitcase rollers moved again with soft complaint. "Take care of each other."

Sal was smiling as he exited LAX despite the back-up of traffic and the crushing smell of exhaust. Still, it was early; the sun was struggling through the marine layer. He was alive. For how much longer he had no idea, but there was a future ahead of him – *for* him – one that was unexpected, undefined, unknowable, thrilling. Whether there was one for him and Eduardo – who could say? All he was sure of was that, right now, he needed coffee – strong, dark coffee – and he knew a great place in West Hollywood where he could get exactly what he wanted.

# # #

Acknowledgements

This book is a work of fiction. Any similarities to persons living or dead *blah blah blah,* etc. That said, it'd be remiss not to point out that **The NAMES Project Foundation** for the **AIDS Memorial Quilt** does not simply allow one to place their quilt piece wherever they choose. For more information about **The NAMES Project Foundation**, donations for its preservation, or how to create your quilt, please go to www.aidsquilt.org/.

Patchwork would not have been written without the immeasurable mentoring, genius, patience and, yes, friendship of John Rechy. His *City of Night* is a seminal classic that inspired many people who came of age both in a pre- and (let's hope) post-AIDS world; and his own *The Coming of the Night* is a gripping, heartbreaking work set at the dawn of AIDS that reads like an unstoppable thriller.

Many thanks to many people: Charles Degelman, for remembering my work and bringing it to the good folks at Harvard Square Editions, Ltd.; Don Weise, who admired a novella called *Patchwork* and encouraged me to turn it into a full-length novel; writing teachers of the past — George Chambers, John Augustine, and Eve La Salle Caram — all of whom left an indelible mark; Jose Chacon, for the amazing artwork — maybe next time!; the best Greek chorus of Aunts — Marie, Rosie, Henrietta, and Josephine; Kim Wiles, the best listener and most voracious reader in the world; Flora Degeorge, for ongoing friendship and general awesomeness; Lori Guggenheim, for just getting it; Stacy Deckard, for the last-minute help; and a cadre of exacting readers whom never tired of scouring endless revisions to improve a tough-minded novel with limited commercial prospects: J. L. Morin, Chris Rice, Wendy Masri, Len Leatherwood, and too many more to mention.